Diary of a Middle-Aged Mermaid

K. L. Laettner

ALSO BY K. L. LAETTNER

TALES FROM THE THRIFT

There are always a million things that going into the creation of a story. Thoughts and memories filter through the mind when the muse speaks, and so many times I listen. Whispered names and places, some of which I've never seen or known, swirl in my mind and spill themselves out on to these pages that you will read.

Thank you to everyone who supports me in making my dreams come true, from Jeffery, my number one fan, to the souls in the internet land, who listen to my tirades and share in the snippets as I clip along on this journey, to family and close friends, and so many more.

I could list a thousand of you here, and it would take an entire book just to mention all of your names. For the wonderful photographer, Terri Cnudde, who captured her beautiful daughter on a beach, to Lana Mowdy, who beat the clock to edit my chaos, to the places mentioned in the book that I frequent often; and to the women who taught me through their own hard learned lessons, how to believe in myself and rise up.

I hope you enjoy this story as much as I do.

Born of love and belief in living a beautiful life, one stroke at a time, we will continue swimming forward.

Thank You

Dedication

This book is dedicated to every person who found their strength through adversity, and in doing so, made the choice to rise and become all that they dreamt possible. In life we will witness both love and loss. How could we not? For it is what life is made of.

As we reach for all we desire, we will surface to find paradise through the infinite possibilities that twinkle like stars above us.

"I don't really want to become normal, average, standard. I want merely to gain in strength, in the courage to live out my life more fully, enjoy more, experience more. I want to develop even more original and more unconventional traits"

— *Anaïs Nin*

Chapter One

                                                                          1

Chapter Two

                14

Chapter Three

                21

Chapter Four

                28

Chapter Five

                34

Chapter Six

                44

Chapter Seven

                53

Chapter Eight

                68

Chapter Nine

                76

Chapter Ten

                83

Chapter Eleven

                93

Chapter Twelve

                98

Chapter Thirteen

                106

Chapter Fourteen

                116

Chapter Fifteen

                131

Chapter Sixteen

141

Chapter Seventeen

154

Chapter Eighteen

164

Chapter Nineteen

175

Chapter Twenty

187

Chapter Twenty One

199

Chapter Twenty Two

207

Chapter Twenty Three

220

Chapter Twenty Four

232

Chapter Twenty Five

242

Epilogue

247

Author Bio

250

Chapter One

A Mermaid is born/ beautiful graffiti

Summer 1983

Hey Diary,

This is so stupid. The word childish certainly comes to mind, and as far as I'm concerned, I see this whole exercise as pretty damn pointless.

I was discussing my future with my shrink, and I told her I had always wanted to be a mermaid, and she told me to write about it in a diary. What one has to do with the other, I don't know, but here we are, you and me, together at last.

Christ, that sounds so bad, almost like I'm a twelve-year-old kid. In case I royally mess this up, I want you to know that I've never owned a diary. I remember seeing them in the stationery store; this was back in the dark ages when I was a young thing. Those diaries were so cutesy and usually a petal pink color. They always had a little metal latch and a funny looking key to lock them with. But my young smarty-girl senses told me that somehow the chintzy lock wouldn't hold up to a parent who wanted to get a gander at what was inside. They'd find a way. I was convinced; hence, I never saw the need to have one. Secrets are meant to be kept hidden away from view, and what with those big words DIARY etched across the front in big shiny gold letters, what's so secret about that? Right? Might as well write it on a billboard for Christ's sake.

I don't know what to write, but I was told I should start with what I remember about my childhood. It wasn't very exciting, trust me. Hmmm...I ate a Gaines Burger once. I know, not quite the showstopper you were expecting. So, I'm sure you'd be thinking, why the hell would I eat a dog food hamburger meant for fluffy, right? Because my little sister dared me to; that's why. I couldn't not do it once I was dared to; it was protocol for kids.

It was nasty. I remember it was like chewing rubber. I found it a bit salty, and those little orange bits that resemble cheese taste nothing like their look-a-like cheddar counterpart. The point is that I rose to the challenge and I did it. Granted, I puked a few minutes later, but Harmony had to pay me a buck, so that was totally worth it in my eyes. I was maybe eight or nine, and God knows we were all clueless at that age. Mom told us that we don't gain very many smarts until we reach the double digits, if ever. I don't think that dog food was the purpose of writing in you.

Time to get a little more specific, so I guess this entry will start down at the local drugstore. It was back when I had to shop for a gift for my teacher for Christmas. Don't ask me why; it's just the second thing that pops into my mind. I ate Play-Doh once, too. I shaped it like peanut butter cookies and even used a fork to make the little tine marks on top, and let me just say, fresh and squishy or dried and crumbling, Play-Doh is some nasty tasting stuff, makes the Gaines burger taste like candy. I'm all about the food. Why do I keep going back to the food?

Crap, I'm getting off topic again. So, the drug store tale, back to that. I've always been one to trust my first feeling, and I'm not saying that that feeling was always correct. It was mostly wrong for me most of the time, but why buck the trend?

It was cold outside. Winter in Buffalo was always frigging cold, fact of life, folks. I remembered at the last minute that I was supposed to pick up a gift for my teacher. Of course, I blurted it out after dinner, right before the Wonderful World of Disney was to start. I always looked forward to that show, but I didn't want to walk in tomorrow without a gift and look like a jerk.

The snow was falling in those big fluffy chunks that add up fast, and I was bundled up like there was a blizzard coming. Mom could be paranoid at times, and she must have felt that she couldn't let me freeze to death. Yep, having to drive that whole two blocks to the drugstore with my father, I could get hypothermia or something. The car never warmed up for such a short drive, so in hindsight, I guess it made sense. Buffalo equals f'ing freezing in my mind, and I think it still is for most of the year. Blame it on global warming but in reverse for the North; no warming for you up there. All you get is just cold, cold, and more f'ing cold. I don't live there anymore so I can say that.

The windows of the store were all steamed up, with thin lines of water running like a river down the glass. It marred the view of the snowmen scene they had set up as the window display. It looked as if poor old *Frosty* had already turned into the puddle, minus the pretty poinsettias and sweet little Karen. No, I didn't forget about Hocus-Pocus the rabbit, but there would be no rabbits in the window until Easter...which comes to the stores right after Christmas.

I was set free to roam the store once we walked through the two sliding doors that sloshed open. Big gobs of half-melted snow kept them from fully closing once you walked through. My feet were equipped in big moon boots. They were pretty snazzy but only worked in normal winter temps, not this fifteen below wind-chill stuff. Just forget about using a cart too. They were all out in the corral covered with a foot of snow or frozen in place like an apocalyptic scene at the outskirts of the lot. If you did manage to drag one in, your hands would never warm up if you were holding that ice-cold metal handle on your trek through the store.

I was waddling up and down the aisles, my snow pants making that nylon on nylon rubbing sound as I moved, and my pants beneath the winter wear would begin bunching up my legs, and it pissed me off. But the view before me took my mind off my wardrobe problems as I stared at everything as if it were my first time allowed in a store. My mouth was open wide, and I gawked at the holiday decorations, transfixed by all the sights and smells of the season.

I love candles that smell like cookies, bayberry, vanilla, and apple pie, that festive holiday scent that makes you remember days when people were kinder and filled with holiday joy. It was more fun back then, when Christmas things came out after Thanksgiving and not in July. We never had holiday burnout back then. It was short-lived, but we looked forward to it. We were grateful for any gifts we received, and we looked forward to the big Sears Christmas catalog that came out. We'd dog ear the pages, showing our parents everything we desired. If we got just one of our hoped-for things, we'd be tickled pink.

Now, meh...I get sick of Christmas by Halloween. The seasonal items were always such a kick to me, and oh, how they loved to put the cheap shit down low where us little kids could get up close and personal with it. We could touch it, smell it, and pester our parents to buy it. Did I mention the gingerbread man candle? Boy, he made my mouth water.

Back to the store. As you can see, I'm like a hound dog with a squirrel. Focus, Destiny, focus. I found the cosmetics aisle and all the pretty boxes that were decorated for Christmas that called to my girly sense of awe. It was there that I spied them. Jars of round rainbow-colored jelly bath ball thingies that were scented like...I don't know what, and to this day, I still can't describe it.

That scent was on some woman who passed me recently on the street, and it stopped me in my tracks. Was she wearing it or something? All I know is it was just a God-awful strange smell, and I hope it disappears into the portals of history, like Happy

Days bubble gum cards, strawberry shortcake dolls, and things like that. Some things were just not supposed to be around forever.

So back to those bath balls. Supposedly, they changed the bath water to whatever color ball you put in the water, and it made oily colorful scented bubbles. I mean really, who would want to soak in a tub with a yellow jelly ball bouncing around as it deflated itself in the water? Your nice relaxing bath, I would assume, would turn yellow. Soaking in yellow water would make me feel like swimming in urine, and that's something a mermaid would never lower herself to do. No jelly orbs, nor jelly fish for that matter. I fancy myself a mermaid, but when it comes to swimming with things that can maim you or kill you, count me out.

Now, I know you're thinking to yourself, how does a grown fifty-three-year-old woman fancy herself a mermaid, and for that matter, why? Now I will answer that when I get to it, but it's going to take a little explaining first. Trust me, and maybe if I remember, I'll let you know when we're there.

So anyway, back to the colorful bath balls. I picked out one that had a menagerie of rainbow colored balls, all for the low price of $2.99, or maybe $1.99, but what did I care? I wasn't buying it or using it, and keep in mind I must have been around seven or so. My dad bought it because I didn't have any money. I think he suggested it too.

The teacher who would be bestowed with this amazing gift, hmmm…well, she was a living, breathing fossil. Really, there's no other way to describe her except for fossil-like. White thinning hair, eyes set into a face filled with wrinkles upon wrinkles, and she was all hunched over like a T-Rex. When she walked, it was like her arms were too short for her frame, and her breath was as vile as a dinosaur's. No, I don't know what a dinosaur's breath would smell like, but I'm assuming it wouldn't be pleasant. If I'm wrong and you know any better, well then just let me know.

So, here I bestow my prized Christmas gift to my teacher, and for now, let's just call her Miss Hannover. I have to make up a name because, at my age, I don't remember what it really was. So, Miss Hannover has opened all her gifts from us lovely and always well-behaved children, and here I sit feeling all giddy and shit. I'm just so proud of myself, because I saw what all the other kids had gotten her, and it wasn't anything as special as what I was about to gift her with. She finally picks up my almost perfectly wrapped present. She rips the paper off with her quivering fossil fingers and pulls it out of the pretty candy-cane striped wrapping paper that I painstakingly managed to wrap myself. I purposely don't buy odd shaped gifts to this day for the reason of what a pain in the ass it is to wrap it. I rejoiced the day when gift bags were created.

"Oh, how nice, bath beads, how did you know? I love these," she said, a garbled quiver to her voice, and she smiled at me like my gift was the cat's ass. I was so excited. She liked my gift; she really liked my gift. I was a child with a lot of issues with self-esteem (another topic we shall beat with a stick later), and I was just blushing and gushing that she liked it.

We all sat down after the gift opening. We finished our Christmas cookies and punch, talking with whomever would lower themselves to talk to us, and then, Yay! The bell rang out like a happy echo through the hallways. We ran out of class like we were set on fire with a blowtorch. School was officially done for the holidays, and for some reason (perhaps because my memory has always sucked), I had left my book behind in my desk. We had homework to do over school shut-down, and I needed it. I had to go fetch it or not be able to do that chore of boring history homework.

It was one of those old desks where the wooden chair was attached to the desk itself. A one-piece desk that, God forbid, if you were a chunker, you'd never be able to squeeze into it. They had other desks for the heftier kids, but that wouldn't happen to me for many more years, and by then, they had normal sized desks. It was a relic of a thing that seemed to be born of the dark ages. The desk top lifted back on hinges, and you put your pencils inside in the little dish, your ruler, paper, books, and all the other standard crap they made your parents buy that you never used. So, where was I? I had forgotten my book.

My friends were outside waiting for me, because we all walked home together, the whole half block away, barefoot and in the snow and uphill both ways...ha, I'm being funny, okay, maybe not so much.

So, I walk back into Miss Hannover's classroom and she's, of course, long gone. She was a speedy fossil when it came time for quitting, I guess. I go over to my desk, grab my book, and on my way out, I look down at the garbage can next to her desk that's chock full of ripped wrapping paper and ribbons that were hanging out like festive snakes, and what do I spy? My most amazing present, those precious bath beads that I had spent my parents' hard-earned money on.

The bitch threw out my bath beads! I began rationalizing it with my tiny little pea-sized brain, that maybe they had fallen off of her desk and landed there in the trash. Then I realized that, when she had opened them, she was on the other side of the desk. I would like to say that, at this point, I was crushed, that my little lip quivered in heartbreak, but I'd be lying. Okay, I was a teensy bit crushed, but kind of elated now, too, because I could keep them. I pulled them out of the trash and tucked them into my book bag and carried my precious prize home.

I told myself that day, never again would I buy some miserable teacher any gift; maybe an apple would be my limit after that, and if they had diabetes or something, well, then, tough shit. I know, you're thinking what seven-year-old would speak like that? Just so you know, I would swear when I was little and could get away with it if my parents didn't catch me, and I was quite proud of only having had my mouth rinsed out with Lava soap once. But when no one's around, I can swear like a drunken sailor or perhaps just a feisty mermaid.

So here I have a jar of rainbow bath beads, something my parents would never buy for our household. I obviously can't use them without getting caught, but I thought they were kind of pretty all smushed up together in their little plastic jar. They were a rainbow of perpetual captivity to my young happy eyes. I saw a SpongeBob episode once later in my life. It was where his eyes were filled with huge red hearts, and they were oozing such joy. I knew that look. I had that look when I looked at my rainbow ball jar. I was in love with their bright happy colors.

You've got to understand; things weren't always normal in our house. We could only use the liquid potion that Mom picked out for our rare bubble baths. It was only later that she outlawed it, because us girls were told "we'd get diseases in our privates if we soaked in bubbles," her words, not mine. Maybe she learned it on Dinah Shore or the Phil Donahue show. I don't know where she got half of her "current and up to the minute" information from. To this day, at my ripe old age, I still refuse to use bath bombs, bubbles, or anything that may get my privates diseased. What the hell were our parents thinking, I often ask myself.

So, we were lucky enough back then to get the Mr. Bubbles stuff, even after my mother got a look at the freaky commercial. In the Mr. Bubbles commercial, there was this creepy guy who kind of looked like Gilligan (the dimwit man/boy of the shipwrecked three-hour tour show), and he was sitting in a big tub of bubbles. As he held pink balloons and rose up out of the water, his body is covered in bubbles (thank God), but then they start popping, and you think you're going to see this hairy-legged naked dude drifting out of the tub. We watched him go higher and higher, unable to turn away, like watching a train wreck about to happen. I was a kid, and it freaked me out in a strange "something is seriously wrong with this guy" kind of way. Then the little jingle plays, Mr., Mr. Bubbles...Pop... hahaha...(the little kids behind the scenes in the commercial would laugh hysterically), and my mom grimaced, shaking her head back and forth as she stalked over to change the channel, a cigarette hanging out of the corner of her mouth and a cup of coffee clenched tight in her fist. (Back then, you still had to get off your ass and change the channel or have your kids do it.) Kids were cheap labor back then, really cheap. I think she was worried it would offend our delicate girly senses. I'm surprised I remembered it. Maybe talking to you is helping me to focus and remember things after all.

So, back to the beads. I didn't want to tell my folks that my teacher was a douche-bag, not that I knew what one was back then, but I sure as heck do now. I was mortified, and I didn't want to get Miss Hannover in trouble. I needed to get good grades, even if sucking up to a teacher was the only way I'd get them. I hid the pretty ball-filled jar in my room on the windowsill behind the yellow and white checked curtains. I liked how the colors looked with the sun shining on them, the rainbow prism on the walls effect.

Well, somewhere along the way, I kind of forgot about them, and now you'll see how often I cleaned my room, too.

When spring comes along in Buffalo, it turns the bitterly ice cold to not quite warm, then to maybe spring or it will skip it altogether and go directly to hot and sweaty summer. Then the rains fall, a lot, and still those little beads are sitting in their plastic jar, sad and unloved, turning themselves into a strange kind of volcanic science project.

At some point in time, the lid had blown off after the cheap plastic seal holding it down decomposed, and when the rains came, those little bath beads turned into expanding mutant foamy rivers, running colors down the side of our sparkling white siding from the second story window.

I don't know who saw it first, but it wasn't a pretty sight. Well, it was to me, but my butt wasn't so pretty afterwards. I think that was the first time I really got into any serious trouble. The thing was, the folks knew I didn't have any money to buy them, so their first thought was that I five-finger discounted them from down at the pharmacy. Well, don't they just throw me in the car and drag me down there to have a chat with Mr Andrews, the pharmacist who owned the joint.

So, Mr. Andrews stands there and gives me the tongue lashing I didn't deserve. His spittle was flying everywhere like a monsoon was hitting with its full-frontal wetness. He was bitching about how kids these days were hellions, our lack of common manners, the whole shebang, and I just stood there in my mightier than thou, head held high Super Girl attitude and took it. I think I even imagined that I was wearing a cape to ward off the viscous verbal attack, you know, bounce that venom right off my magnificent self. I had a great imagination when I was young, by the way, and here I was, fighting for the justice of a seven-year-old's world, and by golly, I was going to win.

He asked me if I had anything to say for myself, and of course, at this point, all I could muster up was "that they just magically appeared there in my window, that I hadn't stolen a thing, thank you very much; now if you'll excuse me, I'll just leave now." See, I was polite about it. I smiled sweetly, and he turned crimson as his veins protruded from the sides of his neck. He looked like his head was going to explode like a big red balloon.

He put his hand on my shoulder as I turned away, and thank heavens my parents intervened, or I may have socked him in the balls. I was always told, if a man ever grabbed you, aim for the jewels. It's bad enough that, at my height, that's what my view was, and I certainly wasn't impressed. So, my parents shuffled me back home, ignoring me for the whole short ride, and when they pulled in, I jumped out of the car and stormed into the house, slamming the door behind me.

I remember hearing that I was grounded for two weeks, and that I'd have to help clean up the mess. They wouldn't let me climb a ladder, mind you, yet would let us all out onto the roof to watch fireworks every summer, and you wonder why we're so screwed up as adults.

So, now I'm grounded. It's summer vacation, and they take away my bike. I told them I hadn't stolen the bath beads, but they didn't believe me, so, case closed. I was a victim of the f'd up parental justice system. The rainbow flow made it all the way to ground level, so I was able to scrub that portion off, and then when the dye wouldn't come out, I helped with painting over it. My beautiful mermaid hair inspired graffiti was no longer. I was sorry to see it go, but the neighbors were happy we were no longer lowering their home values.

I never did tell them where the beads came from, but then I was never stupid enough to put anything on a windowsill again. But they were pretty, the way they flowed down the side of the house in their foam-dripping glory. I can see it still in my mind, how it looked like long tendrils of mermaid hair. It could be where it all began. An artist and mermaid wanna-be was born.

Chapter Two

A Mermaid Sins...And the controversial art of terrorizing boys

Dear Diary,

I honestly can't comprehend why I still talk to you, except for happily discovering it to be somewhat fun. The old gray matter is recollecting things that, up until this time, had only festered in the sticky cobwebs of my disordered mind. Many cobwebs exist up there, and heaven knows tidying was never my strong suit. God only knows what else may fall out before I'm done.

I vaguely remember events from my childhood, for better or worse. One can only swim in the imperfectness of memories for so long before being pulled under in their current. Often times, it may be better to grab hold of something when I can, and now that's your job, so hello, life preserver. Hopefully, you enjoy listening to me prattle on, because it encourages me to keep writing.

I had gone away to overnight summer camp, earth shattering news, right? This is a few years after my mermaid hair flowing down the house incident. It is where I may have fastened lips with a boy, or I should say, he kissed me. It is also the first time I may have accidentally struck a boy in his nuts hard enough that he had to seek medical attention. Don't worry. I'll get to the story before we are through.

So, at this point, I am sitting at a church camp. It's not my first venture at a camp but the one I really enjoyed most. It's the first time I felt accepted by other kids my age. We'd go to a big gazebo-style shelter at night where we would sing uplifting songs. They would pass out these thin blue books that contained all the lyrics. Everyone knew the songs except for me; it was my first time there. We'd gather after a laborious day of playing in the sun, and we'd sing. We did it with such gusto, loudly and sometimes off key, and we laughed. I still recall that part most, the laughter.

Religious stories were recited between songs, and even though I had gone to vacation bible schools, these lessons seemed on a more mature level. They didn't regard us as little kids. We were becoming young adults. I would look around at all of their smiling faces, my dearest friend beside me. We would sing merrily and listen to the fantastic tales or what were more likely parables that engaged our open-minded senses. It was a glorious time for me, but also the first I can recall sinning on purpose. I know precisely what you're thinking to yourself. Why would this innocent and beautiful child sin? I shall get to it momentarily.

An honorable mention of meditation time is needed first. At mid-day, we'd go down and sit by the lake. You were given a thin notebook and a sheet of paper filled with open-ended questions. Things like:

What is something you are grateful for?

What is it that you love most in this world?

What do you want to be when you grow up?

I would meditate (that's what they dubbed it) over what should have been pretty easy questions. The hardest part was that we couldn't sit by anyone. We sat stoic and isolated, meditating over our futures, and I looked at the others and wondered what divine inspiration they were coming up with. It was calming and peaceful in its extraordinary way, so credit goes to whomever decided to chill us out in this creative manner. It was what kind of geared me into who I would become later in life.

"I want to be a Mermaid" was my defiant answer. I'd stare out at the rippling waves where the sunlight reflected like diamonds and picture myself out there somewhere. Within my daydream laden mind, I swam in the company of dolphins and became one with the ocean. Let's completely overlook the fact that it was a lake; no dolphins would ever be seen there, but one could still pretend.

We had to turn in our sheets after the half-hour had passed, and that's when I had second thoughts. I knew they'd laugh or think I was bullshitting them. I was now unsure. I was being honest, really I was, but now I'm second guessing myself. I was never asked about my response, but they did hover closer and try to include me more into their little tribe. Perhaps they thought I was crazy. Who knows? I just wanted to be truthful.

Evening was the time for our beloved sing-a-long. I had waited for it in a giddy kind of excitement, but it still bothered me that I could never recollect all the words. I remembered feeling amazing as we performed each song, our voices coming together in exquisite harmony. I wanted to take that home, that feeling. I wanted to sit in my room, singing those songs of praise from that magical blue book and just feel that goodness wash over me. Those songs were reminiscent of my rainbow balls, tucked into a jar and meant to last forever. The lyric book was a captive opus of goodness.

I stole that blue book, tucking it away in a notebook. I looked around to see if anyone had seen me, but everyone was just praising Jesus and singing Hallelujah. I breathed in deep and smiled. I had gotten away with it.

Once back at my cabin, I tucked it away beneath my bunk in my miniature suitcase. I had now become a thief at Jesus camp. Jesus would be okay with my pilfering, because it's the only way I'm going to remember the songs. When I got back home, I could sing him praises. That made it okay, right?

I tried being logical about the whole thing, but when I got home and slid it out, I was just ashamed of myself. I slipped the book in the Sunday newspaper after everyone was done reading it and buried it between the pages then tucked it in the garbage. I couldn't stand the uncomfortable reminder of my sin. I think about it often and wish I would have kept it. There were some excellent songs in there.

Ergo, while riding on the old sin train to Hell, the next big faux pas I mastered was with the charming boy who kissed me. It was witnessed, much to my dismay, by the town crier. Boys and girls alone together in lodging areas at camp was a huge no-no. I'm sure it was thrilling for his royal cuteness, but it didn't end as peacefully for the other boy. In hindsight, I must say, tattle-tales never prosper, and shit happens.

You see, when I was younger, you would have found me to be a bit tomboyish. On that eventful day, I had just discovered a perfect tree to climb. It was just minutes after the kissing event. I was doing well on my ascent. I sat high like an eagle, surveying the lands below. That nasty little boy decided he wanted to get all up in my face about being alone with the cute one. Jealous little prick, I thought to myself, before wondering just how much trouble this might get me in.

He taunted me with petty words and then began meandering his way towards me. Climbing up one overhead branch then another, his intent clear. He was hell-bent on attempting to pry me out of my majestic perch. His grubby hand grasped my slender ankle, and he pulled like I was a rope in tug-of-war. I lost my grip and came sliding down, with the little turd falling not so gracefully down below me. He hit the ground hard, stood up, then started yelling at me for pushing him out of the tree.

I'm falling down while trying to seize branches and stop myself. Somewhere within, I found my super teenage girl strength and grasped onto the lowest branch before hitting the hard ground. But alas, for the boy-child, fate was about to deliver the cruelest blow. He stood below me, his face distorted and beet red as his shrill voice screamed at me; my body was still in movement from the distance I had fallen.

It was then that it happened. I was magically transformed into Nadia Comaneci, swinging from the last branch with my sinewy muscles born of tree climbing and cleaning mermaid soap hair off the house. I was swinging through like I was preparing for a Japanese dismount on the uneven bars. I held on to that branch for dear life, and he moved out of the way as fast as a sloth on sleeping pills. I connected. BAM! Right in the jewels.

Now keep in mind; it was never and under any circumstances my intention to injure the insignificant bastard; it was just an unexpected accident. He never did tell on me, as I did enlist help for him. The ambulance showed up a short time later and hauled him away.

Lesson learned, don't get caught kissing boys, and never, ever steal a songbook from church camp. As for the boy who kissed me, the following day, I caught him kissing my best friend behind his cabin in a wooded area. I suppose it was an eye-opener and a lesson about trust all in one.

Mitch, his name just screams entitled wealthy boy. He was good looking, with that air of rich-parental money swirling about him. Mitch of the perfect Lacoste alligator shirt, Sperry shoes, and perfectly coiffed feathered hair. It might have been a glaring clue to me if I'd been paying attention. It is possible the lesson was not to date extremely attractive boys. I graduated out of church camp a little wiser. I learned you can't depend on anyone, especially boys, and you should never steal or tell a lie…or kick boys in the jewels if it can be prevented.

I don't ever recall being invited back to that camp after that.

Chapter Three

A sirens song of guilt/ always remember where the wine is hidden.

Dear Diary,

I'm getting used to this now, and I think I'm doing okay at it. You haven't told a soul, and that's one point of this exercise. I guess I should thank my shrink for recommended you to me, and although you're not one of those cutesy pink diaries of my youth, your cover is pretty darn cool, and I find, with your blank pages, it encourages me in a pathetic way to fill you up; maybe then this chore can be done. When you're done, maybe I can then be done.

Now my intent is not to shock you, although that may come later. I guess it depends on how ballsy I feel. So, fast forward past the childhood of summer camps, church and otherwise. I guess the next drop in our way back machine would be to around the fourteen or fifteen-year-old age segment. I was still dreaming of mermaid-hood, but with the lake so far away from where I lived and having to sit in school every day, it kind of put the kibosh on thinking about it as much.

I was still learning the ways of the world, trying to stay out of trouble, and then I met a new girl at school. She was younger than me, prettier than me, much, much larger boobs than me, and for additional bonus points, her sister could buy us beer.
When we first practiced the art of being all grown up, we trifled with some really crappy booze. Linda of the generous cha-chas had stolen some Sloe Gin and some Creme De Menthe from her parents' liquor cabinet. She figured, with the dust on the bottle, they'd never miss the stuff.

We'd go out on a Friday night, hang out behind the police station in the woods (figuring the best place to party was right below their noses), and meet the rest of the kids who would show up with a variety of beverages. I think we did it because we knew it was wrong, but the feeling of rebellion, when all week long we were good little girls and boys, was just too tempting.

We smuggled the bottles to the get-together in our overstuffed backpacks. The booze and legally bought smokes were tucked up into our sweatshirts for safe keeping. We couldn't let the bottles smash together. The glass on glass sound alone would give us away.

Pretending to go into our destination once we were dropped off, we would instead, round the corner to where the path was to the woods. Once in a while the cops would be sitting there as if waiting to catch us, and if so, we'd turn around slowly, decked out in our skin tight Jordache jeans and brown chukka boots with the red laces and pretend like we weren't actually heading that way. Sometimes they would pull up, ask a few questions, then drive off. We'd go into a store in the plaza, kill some time, and then sneak back and meet up at the party.

Well, the next thing I know, we're passing the bottles around. One was a green liquid and one a bright red. I honestly don't remember how much of it I drank, but the next thing we know, they're both empty. Some guy handed me a beer. It was piss warm at best, but beggars can't be choosers. Linda and I left the party when things started getting a little crazy. We just wanted a place to hang out, not to get arrested.

I'm carrying my can of cheap warm beer, and as we walked along, there was a big puddle in between the buildings where we had to get through. Linda asked me if she could have a sip of my beer, having drunk all of her own. Between staggers, I handed it to her. Doesn't she bring it up to her mouth, take a swig, and then proceed to drop it right into the big puddle. So, here am I, being what I considered at the time the smarter of the two. I drop to the ground lightning fast and try to rescue the beer before it can get any water mixed in it. I'm looking at this big-ass puddle and realize that a slew of delivery trucks must have driven through it. The rainbow-colored oil sheen was rippling on the top as plain as day. More mermaid colors, I thought to myself, and took a big swig of the beer anyway.

So, I realize it tastes kind of funny, and the next thing I know, I'm retching my guts out all over the wall of the building. We've now gone from mermaid hair on the wall of my childhood home to red and green with god knows what mixed in, all dripping down like a bad graffiti artist's work all over the side of the building. It was in my hair, on my clothes, everywhere. My girlfriend starts laughing like a maniac, and low and behold, here comes the police car.

I managed to walk away, trying to look as innocent and as sober as I could, and they passed us by with a quick glance our way. We held our breath while waiting for them to turn around and cart our asses off, but they never stopped. Maybe they just didn't want vomit in their car. I never felt so lucky in my life.

After that fiasco, I swore off hard liquor, but wine was next on the docket. My innocent (I say this with an eye roll) friend Linda decides that, the next time, I've got to bring the booze. So, the weekend rolls around again, and with my folks not being big drinkers, I could only find a gallon jug of Lake Niagara in the garbage closet. Again, the dust on the bottle told me I'd be pretty safe pilfering a little. The biggest dilemma was what to put it in. I couldn't steal the whole thing, and besides, we couldn't drink that much anyway, and to be greedy, well, that would just be wrong.

So, I put my getting smarter by the year pea brain into deep thought mode and came up with the idea of thermoses. The old school lunch boxes that we used when we were little kids came with a thermos. You had a cup to drink your stuff out of and it wouldn't spill. So, I scoured the cupboards, deep diving in the back corners where the relics could be found. I was long past the days of using a lunch box but managed to come up with two thermoses, both with a dancing Snoopy on them.

I waited for my big break when I wouldn't get caught and then poured wine into both of them. I hid them away in my room until it was time to leave for the roller rink; that's where we said we were going that night. I wiped the dust off the gallon bottle. I explained to my mother after I was done sweeping out the closet that it was quite dirty in there. I couldn't leave my fingerprints on it after disturbing the dust, and I thought I was pretty smart to cover my tracks.

We drank the small amount of wine that I had pilfered and then it ran out. Again, we were given some warm beers by the boys. They were older than us, and I suppose they thought they'd get somewhere if they plied us with enough alcohol. Alas, it never worked out that way for them. The hormones hadn't kicked in fully yet, I guess. So, we have our fun and then at the Cinderella witching hour, her dad comes to gets us, and he drops me off back at my house. I get up to my bedroom and then I felt that sinking "oh shit" feeling hit me in the gut. I had left the backpack with the thermoses in his car.

I was freaking out, afraid of her folks finding it and being grounded for life. I called Linda right away and told her to get it out of there, because they'd see the thermoses and smell the wine in them and we'd be up a shit creek without a paddle. She ran out and retrieved the bag then brought it back to me on her bicycle the next day. Of course, my mom was out in the yard gardening as she pulled up. I took the bag from her and ran it up to my room, where I proceeded to hide the thermoses beneath all my winter sweaters that lived in my old toy box. They were just hanging out there until I could find time to clean them without being caught. Of course, there goes my memory again. I told you about my cleaning skills or lack thereof, right?

Three or four months later, my mom is doing something in my room, putting something away or changing our clothes over for the season, and she finds the thermoses. The wine had been festering in there for months now and had some pretty green mildew growing on it from mouth bacteria. I always aced my science projects.

So, I come in from school, and here are these two sad-looking little thermoses with a happy dancing Snoopy on them. They were sitting on the counter, and my mother looked pissed. There would be no happy dancing with her. She stood leaning against the counter, a cigarette hanging out of her mouth and with "that" look on her face. I could have sworn she was about to turn into the Incredible Hulk. It took me a few nano-seconds to realize why, but when I did, my terror notched up ten-fold.

How does one explain to one's mother that she isn't perfect, that she makes mistakes, and that she thinks she's gone insane? She didn't buy it, and I'm sure that, when she was my age, she probably did stupid shit too, but yet again, I was grounded and not allowed to go out on weekends with my friends for a month. But I think that's okay. It gave my liver a fighting chance to heal up from all that abuse, but sitting around to watch movies on family night wasn't exactly what I had in mind for punishment. Yea old family night, now that was a punishment, in and of itself.

After that incident, her sister was wheedled into buying us beer. She let us pick our poison, and mine was always Lowenbrau, and I don't know, but I don't think mermaids should really drink beer. They should have fruity cocktails with little umbrellas in it; they can sip them all dainty-like as they sit soaking up the sun at the swim up bar with their mermaid girlfriends. They can tell jokes, wear scale screen to keep from burning, and watch all the mermen swim by. I'll have to add that to my bucket list. Remind me, okay?

Chapter Four

The mermaid gets chunky/ A whole dozen donuts? Where?

Dear Diary,

Thanks for listening. I know by now you must be thinking that I'm such a bad person. I'm not though, trust me. Now, where was I?

Back around the same time as the alcohol shenanigans, I weighed in at around 102 pounds. All through high school, I never budged from that weight. I had been told often that I was as skinny as a rail, a "tit-less wonder" according to the boys, and that I had absolutely no ass.

I had a job babysitting, and before you even think about it, please know that I took my job seriously enough that I never had friends over or drank while any child was in my charge. The pay was good too; although these days, I hear they're just killing it with what they charge. I'm glad my days of needing a sitter are long gone. I was the sitter for Leila for the most part, unless we had a work affair to attend for Alec, then we hired the sitting out to a neighbor lady.

Back then, having a job meant that I had a steady flow of money for the first time ever in my pockets, to spend however I saw fit. I had grandiose plans of banking it until I was a millionaire, but when I did the math, I realized that it would take too damn long. Besides, there were things a young girl just had to have.

I'd go down to the local Woolworths and buy cassette tapes on clearance or some candy or some makeup that I wasn't allowed to wear. There was no Maybelline or Cover Girl for me. My first blush and eyeliner were dirt cheap and probably looked it. I was a *Seventeen* magazine failure when it came to following beauty buying advice.

I think I developed my sweet tooth around that time, now that I think about it. I favored red licorice or anything that was Swedish jelly fish-like in consistency. Gummi bears were also a favorite. A half-pound Hershey bar with almonds was the ultimate in splurge, costing maybe $1.50 or less. But donuts, mmm...now donuts were my downfall. In our home, they were a confection always reserved for a special breakfast treat.

So, wouldn't you know it? The Boy Scouts or some other young guy group is selling donuts. It was to be a baker's dozen (that's thirteen of them, in case you were unsure, because I didn't know that until I opened the box), and they were from a place called Freddie's or something like that.

I was always paranoid about getting into trouble after the wine thing, and I know what you're thinking...girl, didn't you learn anything? But come on, these were donuts, a far cry from something that could seriously impair you.

Five bucks would buy you a box of these freshly made, still warm glazed donuts. Come to think about it, it was summer and hot, so maybe that's why they seemed warm. They were to be delivered three weeks after you placed your order. I forked over my money and waited in anticipation for my prized donuts. I had the date circled on my calendar. Ooh, it was going to be a good date, me and my donuts...together at last.

These donuts were heaven, think Crispy Kreme, but much bigger (donuts on massive steroids). My girlfriend's brother brings them over on the day they received them for distribution, and of course, my mom is again hanging around. I swear she always seemed in my mind, intent on busting my grand schemes with those eyes in the back of her head senses.

I couldn't tell her I had blown five bucks on donuts. I don't know why. I still wonder to this day, would it really have been such a big deal? I had to smuggle them in the house and up to my bedroom. I put them on the shag rug on the floor in my closet and covered them up with a puffy down comforter. It was summer then, and the blanket was not needed, and it made a perfect cover to hide my contraband goodies.

Well, here I am, an Uber-light 102 pounds, and then here's this big yummy smelling box of glazed donuts. They were sitting there festering in my closet and calling my name every time I went into my room. I don't remember when I realized it. I just knew. My butt was expanding. Baby was getting some "back."

Pardon the graphic nature of this, but before the donut incident, I could see the sides of the seat next to my skinny little toothpick thighs when I sat on the toilet. I was small, thin legs, and did NOT take up the whole seat. I swear to God. But I ate that entire box of donuts in three days or maybe less. I think by then I was so sick of them that I may have left a half a donut in the box, so twelve and a half big, juicy glazed donuts…and of course, another science project was born, this time with the addition of ants. Plus, the big ole' butt. Shocking!

So, I'm busy that summer, playing tennis, swimming every day, riding my ten speed. I was an active little thing (please, don't ask me what happened to her. I'm still trying to unearth her below all of this drama), and one day, I'm all hot and sweaty, and I realize that up until this time, my sweat never had an odor to it. But as I cleaned the inside of the car windows on that hot summer day, I was dripping wet, and worse yet, I stunk. I didn't know what was happening to my body. Big butt and B.O. It sounds like a railroad, BB & BO, all aboard!

I hadn't quite reached that most wonderful time in a young girl's life when that Queen bitch Mother Nature shows up and kills it for the next twenty-five plus years. So, in the course of what seems a week, I now have to shower daily, and when I sit on the throne, I can no longer see the edges. My butt and hips have grown, and I am getting fat. My legs and butt have taken over, and I was feeling large and not in charge. I was not happy about it at all.

I told my mother what was happening, and I think she laughed. I don't recall. I think she called them "child-bearing hips" and handed me her tube of roll-on deodorant to use until she could buy me my own. All I know is that it wasn't any fun anymore, and I knew then that things were changing for me. Then "they" started to grow, and now I'm now mortified at the need for a training bra. The neighbor lady had tweaked my ta-ta's one day and told me I was growing up. I wanted to smack her but was too embarrassed to do or say anything. I heeded the advice of my mother and watched for other presents to arrive.

I continued to swim every day. When I was beneath the bright blue water, I was thin again. I had no worries, no concerns, just me in the deep blue. I'd flip my mermaid legs like a dolphin uses its tail. I held them closed tightly together, moving fluidly, and I'd surface up out of the water to the sight of a summer sun…and a lifeguard that was really, really cute. All of a sudden, my mermaid legs were growing hairs, and they would have to be shaved, lest it slowed me down while I swam or I was mistaken for Sasquatch.

I guess with the burgeoning curves that summer came the hormones in hot pursuit. Damn donuts, I still blame them for it all. Oh yeah, and Raid works good for ants on moldy donuts in the back of closets. But I never did figure out how to clean off the grease mark that expanded up the wall to about a foot and a half in height. Boxes absorb donut grease, as does a fancy paint job your mom had painstakingly done.

Just don't expect your clothes to smell pleasant for a while. Grease and Raid, not a good combination.

Chapter Five

Mermen on the prowl...the universal attraction, or not

Dear Diary,

    I think this is too impersonal. You and I, we should be on a friendlier level. You need a proper name that isn't plain, old Diary. How does Farrah sound to you? I've loved her since I was a kid, yet I don't fully love you, not yet. You are more like someone's wise aunt, so how about we call you Kate? Yes! Hello there, Aunt Kate. I'm Destiny Montgomery. It's nice to make your acquaintance. Does anyone even say that anymore? Destiny is my real name. I'm supposed to be honest, and I wouldn't lie to you, Aunt Kate. I have no need to give an alias. I am what I am. Popeye explained it so well.

So, now that that's out of the way, I suppose I should move to the next subject that's been swimming around in my head. Circling like a shark is more apt, but it's in there and moving. You never know, some thoughts can be dangerous.

An explanation on my name is in order, I suppose. I like to imagine my mother being into the hippie thing back in the day, but if she ever was, I'm sure it was short-lived. She was never the free love type, if you catch my drift, more like a typical housewife who didn't work at home. She told me once that she had gone to Woodstock. Hmm...and I asked her who she saw playing while there. She told me Elvis rocked the joint. Yep, Elvis at Woodstock, is that so? We weren't the Cleavers, that's for sure, more a very dysfunctional Partridge Family. My sister is named Harmony, and our dog, bless his departed soul, was Karma.

I asked her why she chose that name for me. When I was young, there was no other kid named Destiny at school or any named Harmony either. It made for some interesting one-liners later in life, but it took me years before I was actually proud of it. Harmony was so easygoing, like a song; her title just seemed to fit. She flat out refused to tell me why, so I was left to my own devices, speculating on what would have prompted the flowery sounding name. I'm still wondering. Maybe I shall make up something. It's certainly better than saying that I don't know.

So, I'm re-reading these passages, and I'm seeing a pattern in here. It has something to do with hiding things, lying, and attempting to live like a rebel. What else is a wannabe mermaid supposed to do? I tried to be good, and even now, I look back at the antics and think, meh, that wasn't so bad. So WHY does it bother me so much? I guess that's your job now, to help me in figuring it all out. As you see, I lose track easily, and at some point in time, I'll try to explain. I don't think I'm ready to put it out there in to the wide-open world yet. I'm still kind of settling down the ghosts.

So, the subject, I guess, is mermen. There was a time that I thought they all sucked, and somedays I still do, but not as often or as much. To me, they were all germ and sperm infested boys who only wanted one thing (I can still hear my mother's voice in my head saying those very words, over and over again), and that wasn't going to be happening as far as I was concerned.

My first real kiss was a fiasco. I'm not counting the church camp kiss here; that paled in comparison. It happened at an afternoon house party where someone's parents weren't home, and we preferred to congregate where we had free-reign and privacy.

Well, this ass-hat guy, let's just call him Chip, he wanted to play kissy face with me, and all I wanted to do was escape his clutches. Chip, now he was quite the octopus, arms moving everywhere, grabbing, touching, or at least trying to. He finally got me hemmed into a corner in the dining room. There was no escape. My heart was beating a mile a minute, and I'm thinking to myself that this is going to be so embarrassing. The kiss was kind of sweet for about ten-seconds. He ambled away afterward with a cocky smile across his puss then told the other kids who were hanging out what he'd just done.

He was so proud of himself, probably raising his fist in the air like he'd just scored the winning goal. I thought of him as Conquistador Chip after that. I'm still standing in the dining room, which joined the kitchen by a door, and was kind of listening in (tell me you wouldn't have done the same), and what does the little bastard say?

"She tasted like milk." Well, duh, I had just had a big glass of Nestle Quick; of course, I'm going to taste like milk. I was embarrassed to say the least. Mortified and very pissed off.

Somewhere in my imaginative little mind, I walked into that room that was filled with hormone raging, angst-ridden, unsure kids, and knocked his block off. (I learned that from Lucy on the Snoopy cartoons.) For a moment I felt better. I felt empowered, and then I came out of my daydream of revenge and stood there while the other kids snickered and pointed at me. I longed to crawl into a hole and die.

Let's just say it was a long while before I ever let a boy kiss me again; not that I let him then, there just wasn't a magical trap door available to fall through to escape him.

I ran into Conquistador Chip a few years later, and the prick didn't remember anything about the kissing and telling episode. He's lost his looks at some point, and now he's sporting a balding, lumpy head and a big protruding beer belly. I bet he isn't cornering young innocent girls in corners anymore. He probably couldn't move fast enough.

I think the saddest part is that, all these years later, I'm still playing the same woe-is-me movie over and over in my head. I should have hit him that last time I saw him, but I just laughed at what he had become and walked away with my head held high. Mom would have called it taking the high road. I call it cowardice. I was never one for confrontation on a good day. I was polite that way...or simply weak; the jury's still out on that one.

I think that I needed to be a mermaid to feel mysterious and different from the rest of the girls. I always thought mermaids were these mystical, strong, and beautiful women, and I was nothing. For a sea-dwelling mermaid, the big, wide ocean went on forever. There was always room for escape from any situation. They had long, pretty colorful hair and, best of all, sea-shell bras. I think the sea-shell bras would be very cool. No underwire is a perfect thing as far as I'm concerned. If you eat a dozen donuts and then get bigger, then just go right down to the seashell store and buy the next size up. Good idea? No? Okay then, so back to the sharks, I mean nasty boys.

I took boys with a grain of salt (minus the margarita mix and booze) and tried to keep them at arms' length. Ridicule wasn't my thing, as I had found out with the kissing episode. My ego wasn't big enough, and I couldn't exactly carry a shell around to crawl into when my insecurities reared their ugly heads, so if I didn't involve myself in their stupid boy crap, the better off I was.

Don't get me wrong. Some could be quite nice, but some were the ones my mother warned me about. Hanging onto my golden goodness (the old virginity thing) was of the highest priority, and I was convinced that, in my school, there were only two types of girls: those that did and those that didn't. Beyond that, they fell into every category imaginable.

You had the sport playing lesbians who hung around exclusively with their own tribal kind, the heads who hung out and smoked at the fence with the bad boys, and then the book nerds. I think, if anything, I was a book nerd. Not smart, mind you, but I'd rather read a book than deal with all the high school crap that went along with growing up in a small town. So, I had my preconceived notions of who was who, and I heard all the scuttlebutt about them and myself. I know now that most of it was made up, including the idea of all jock girls being lesbians, but I still thought that it was a particularly cruel environment to be in at the time.

I think, in a strange way, it's kind of similar to what Facebook has become today. You see all these cool things people are doing, and you think, man, they've got it made. But really, do they? Sometimes I'm sure they're showing only what they want you to see. You never see the scars, the sadness behind the bright lights, or the broken souls that are hiding behind the curtains like wayward ghosts in this play called life. Some are honest, and those are the ones I admire. I want to be like those folks, and someday I know I will be. It just takes some time to learn and change.

I'm convinced that we are all insecure. High school did it to us. At some point in our lives, when we realized we could use words to inflict pain to make ourselves look better, I think a lot of us did just that. I know I'm sorry for a lot of the things I have done, but I'm also smart enough to know that you can't go back and change it. You can only start each day with a clean slate and an intention to be better than you were the day before. Oops, I think I'm doing it again, losing track. I'm sorry, Aunt Kate. Where was I?

Awkwardness with boys, high school moments of embarrassment or bullying, those same old things tend to haunt us as we age. It's all in the lies that we tell ourselves to make it all feel better. We're all on this big, old blue marble, spinning our way through the universe. Certainly, it won't kill us to be a little kinder and truthful, right? So why do we have such a hard time with it then?

I met a boy my senior year. He was one of those nice boys, and I was trying to be a nice girl and, for the most part, succeeding. We'd hang out and watch movies, just the kinds of things that friends did. There was no pressure, no hanky-panky, and after a while, I seriously thought that maybe something was wrong with him. All my friends were having sex...or were they really? Joey was always liked by my mom, and even Harmony took a shine to him. I never had a boyfriend, so come prom time, who better to go with than my buddy Joey?

I didn't want to go to the prom because all of "the talk" that you would be expected to "lose it" by then or else be ridiculed the rest of your life or when you went on to college. So, Joey and I practiced kissing one night; this was my idea, not his. We lock lips and do it like we saw in the movies, and let's just say, I wasn't thrilled. He was my friend, and I had no romantic inclinations towards him whatsoever. I had never thought about him in "that" way, and I certainly didn't want to start now. So, we try again. Nope, still nothing registering on the hormonal Richter scale. Well, we just go back to being buddies after that, and then prom night comes around. You go through the motions of that special night: the pictures, the nice over-priced dinner, the corsage pinned on top of your chest that makes you look like you have one floral mountain of a boob, and then the dance. It was lame then, and I'm sure to this day, it still is. But, Joey (the little bastard) had a plan, you'll see...

His buddy Ted was taking my girlfriend Sandy, so we were going to be double dating that night. They pull in to pick me up in this big boat of a car, and I know that you're thinking, here is this huge back seat; uh huh, yep we can figure it all out. But no, that wasn't it. Hiding in the trunk was a big igloo cooler filled with Miller Lite. They were those little pony bottles where three of them might equal a beer. I was thinking to myself, big spenders, those boys. So, we eat dinner, do the dance thing for about ten minutes, then blow off the dance to go down to the beach.

Keep in mind that, back in the eighties, prom gowns tended to be full length. They were soft and silky and very demure, yet still pretty dresses. These days, it seems that the slutty kind is all I keep seeing in Facebook. They certainly don't leave much to the imagination.

I was cool with going to the beach; mermaids love a good wave. The guys were wise enough to bring some blankets, and we pulled off our stockings, kicked off our shoes, and the guys handed out some of these little bottles of beer. The guys chugged them like they had just run a thirty-mile marathon, but us girls were a little better at pacing ourselves. We held our pinkies up, looking as stylish as we could in our wrinkled gowns, as the sun set lower in the sky.

I remember holding my gown up above my knees and walking into the water. My feet were filthy and they itched. Sand fleas do bite. Then of course, I drop my bottle of beer into the water. But I was like the crafty sea-gulls you see in a McDonalds parking lot, and I pulled that beer snatching ninja move. I swiped my arm out and grasped the bottle before it got too far into the water. I thought I was safe…then I took a swig and realized it

41

tasted of Lake Erie dead fish. Now I'm flying out of the water like a mad woman and trying to make it to the bushes to hurl up that fine dinner I had just consumed, as the rest of my posse sat there and had a good laugh at my expense. Joey did come over to help me out, thoughtfully grabbing some napkins to wipe my face on. I was sad. I was mortified yet again, and I wanted to go home. I was not the driver, so that wasn't going to be happening.

Let's not rehash the "I should have known from the oily puddle days." I remembered, but I thought lake water was a far cry from nasty assed parking lot puddles, and I was a little buzzed, mmm hmm...

Sandy and Ted took a walk down the beach while Joey led me back to the blankets. The night was getting cool, and he laid down on the blanket with me, his soft beer breath lips kissing me softly on the cheek, because who would want to kiss dead fish puke mouth, right?

His hands started wandering. I'm feeling a bit tired and buzzed up. Needless to say, the golden goodness was taken care of that night, and in my defense, I don't think I helped much at all, just kind of waited for it to be over. Joey seemed proud of himself, really cocky about the whole thing, and I suddenly realized that I never really knew him at all. What kind of self-respecting guy does that, I'd ask myself. He called me days later and wanted to hang out or most likely to get a repeat performance.

I cut him off like the skin of a fish with a filet knife. I could no longer trust him, and he knew it. Years later, he ended up getting married and having six kids, then divorced, then remarried, and so on. I wish him well, I suppose, because I am turning the new leaf and all.

42

What I never told him is that I got pregnant that night, and on the following day, my mother died. The two worst days of my life all sandwiched together like a big old club with double bacon, except the sandwich would have been much better than that week was.

Aunt Kate,

I want to thank you for listening to this. I know it is a lot to digest, and I think it's helping me. I feel better saying these things not quite aloud, but almost, and these are things that I've never told anyone. Maybe I just needed to clean out my mind's aquarium and flush out all the algae. I need to be able to see out of the glass again. I know that we are trying to do our best, sometimes managing to succeed in the smallest of ways, but at least we try.

But in the end, we all go out like that green flash of light that happens when the sun goes down. Sometimes you're lucky enough to catch a glimpse before it's gone, and sometimes, you can only imagine it was ever really there at all.

Chapter Six

Mermaids get the blues, and fancy suits.

Dear Aunt Kate,

It has kind of a nice ring to it. I really don't want to talk about this, but I think that's why I should. I'll start with the Mom thing. There was no sickness, just an asshole who ran a red light and smashed into her doing fifty miles an hour. It was while she was on her way home from work. We were told that she died instantly, but it still didn't make it any easier. College was pretty much cancelled for me after that. I had to stay home and help out. Mom's sister moved in with us until we got our bearings.

Harmony was still in school, and I was on the verge of graduating. I got a job, one that I considered a "real" job. It was in, what else, a seafood restaurant, and the tips helped us for food money; the insurance she had left behind covered the rest.

There are so many things I wish I would have told her. I guess after it wears on you for a while, you learn to stop beating yourself up over it. I couldn't change things, and I think as any mother knows, even the unspoken words are often still heard. We become masters at reading the soul and in seeing what lies between the lines. We had our dysfunction, but we had our love, too. But here I am, almost out of my teens, at a time in life when girls get ready to spread their wings and fly, and for Harmony and me, there's now no mother to go to for advice. We had my aunt, but she was kind of useless in the mothering department. She had never had children, so she didn't know much about raising them. But as they say, sometimes shit happens, and sometimes it happens fast and hard.

We couldn't Google crap back then. If you wanted information, you went down to the library and looked it up or you asked your mom. That's one aspect of modern day advancement I really do appreciate; google this or that but pray that you're not taken to a porn site. Information at your touch, who would have thought? I graduated, which I found surprising with all the turmoil from losing Mom, and I had Harmony front and center to cheer me on.

I never knew I was pregnant. Mother nature was quite fickle with me, and let's just say, she didn't always come to the dance on time. It was summer time, and the living wasn't so easy, but I was working. This was over a month after prom night. I remember carrying a tray piled up with fried fish platters. It was beer-battered Cod or Haddock; it depended on what they had gotten in that week. I hate the smell of greasy fried fish to this day. The four red-striped bowls of coleslaw were ripe with vinegar and mayonnaise, and the smell was beginning to get to me. It was hot that day, and the A/C at Carl's Catch (that's where I worked) was struggling to keep up with the heat outside. That whole summer was like living in a broiler, as I recall. I felt like I was going to faint, and I turned away from the tray, trying to breathe in some air that didn't reek of grease, and attempted to get my focus back to what I was doing.

The restaurant was right on the lake. I remember looking out at the waves, and it made me want to cry. I wanted to run over and smash through that dirty plate-glass window, dive into the water below, and swim away from there, never to return. To hell with this nasty food and annoying people. I wanted freedom, and I wanted it right then and there. Hormones were doing flip flops on me.

So, here I have this big table for eight, and it's only occupied by two ancient couples. They were all drinking a Tom Collins, and the red cherry was floating around in the melting ice cubes looking like a crimson eyeball. I think they were on their second round of drinks, and the one man had such a big mouth. Really, a non-stop pie hole that wouldn't quit yammering, and he was on his third drink. He was telling the others a dirty joke that I didn't find funny in the least; it was more sexist than anything, and I stood there and waited patiently for him to finish. Destiny, always polite, especially when getting paid to be.

The tray was feeling heavy, and this jerk just kept going and going (I shall dub thee old energizer mouth). The one elderly lady looked up at me in pity. I think she was his wife, and if her look said anything, it was that she wasn't going to be the one to interrupt his diarrhea of the mouth.

The other blue-haired woman turned and looked over at me; her mouth was wide open and her eyes were bugging out in shock. She was staring at the blood that was running down my leg. My panty hose and shoes were drenched, and then I felt the cramping begin. I didn't know what was happening. I slammed the tray down on the table, sending a bowl of coleslaw to its untimely death on the dirty brick floor. Glass and cabbage and carrot slivers were running in a white river towards me and mixing with the blood that was increasing in intensity. The windbag shut up for a second, and then I turned and ran into the bathroom, my thick rubber-soled shoes making squishing noises as I was slipping and sliding back and forth on the greasy and now blood-soaked tile floor.

The windbag's wife followed me to the restroom, and that's when the pain began to rip through me. I felt like someone was tearing my lower extremities out with meat hooks. They called for an ambulance, and there wasn't anyone at home to call. I couldn't remember my aunt's work number, so I rode to the emergency clinic alone. The doctor said it was a miscarriage, but not to worry, because I shouldn't have any problems in the future having children.

I was in shock. All I could smell was rubbing alcohol and fish fry grease. I hadn't even known I had been pregnant. In the timeframe since prom, I had been drinking, smoking, and God knows what else. I think I was relieved, and I know that it's not a nice thing to say, but I was in no position to have a kid at eighteen. I didn't even know if I wanted to be a mother, ever, truth be told. But to be in this situation and not even realize it, it was a little disturbing to me.

47

I felt stupid. I felt so alone, and I was angry at Joey for what he had done. It took me a while to deal with the rage. I held it all in for many years. So, congratulations, Aunt Kate, you're the first one to hear the news. I'm sorry it took all this time to say it out loud. Maybe I wouldn't be where I am today had I vented about it back then.

I know it was early on in my younger life, and I may have been immature about it, but I still felt the need to give it a name. To this day, I still name everything, stuffed animals, cars, snakes that invade my outdoor space, etc...I don't think they could have told at that stage if it was a boy or a girl, and I don't think I'd have wanted to know. But I still felt the need to give it a name. In a tonsillectomy, they will let you take them home in a jar; this though, they won't give it to you to take with you when released. You can't bury it out in the yard next to your dead pets.

I named her Alia. I thought, had she lived, she would have wanted to be a mermaid too, and Alia would be a beautiful name for a goddess of the sea.

So, I'm crying now. I think it's the first time I've shed tears over that day. Mermaids get the blues too, I suppose. I will make a vow that, from here on out, I will tackle any emotions that come up when I write, good, bad, or otherwise. I know, if I don't get all of this out of me, I'm going to shrivel up and die. I need to move forward and live free of this weight I've been carrying. I want to swim in the deep blue and cleanse away all those years of everything that ever made me sad. I want to be honest, and I promise I will do just that.

I'm getting deep here, but around that time, there was something amusing that happened. Like typical life, with the bad will always come some good. I don't know if this is good or not; it was just funny in hindsight.

Summer was still on us, the air always hot and heavy. I was bringing in a steady paycheck, and Carl even gave me the week off with pay after the Alia episode. This little anecdote happened a month after the miscarriage.

My old swimming suit was getting thread-bare, and I knew it was time for an upgrade. Besides, my shells were growing bigger, and I needed a proper suit to contain the girls. Seashell and coconut bras were frowned upon in Buffalo.

A catalog had come in the mail. It was filled with some very pretty swimsuits. It may have been Avon, I'm not sure, but when I opened up that page, ooh…I was in love. I had finally found the perfect suit. I wasn't one for caring how I looked most of the time, but this suit was the bees' knees. It had red and white stripes turning diagonally to minimize the not so thin stomach. The front plunged almost to my belly button, and there were ruffles. I know, ruffles are not good. They are back in these days, I've heard, but back then, not a fashionable thing. But the ruffles fit the design of the suit so nicely. The thighs were cut super high, and the back plunged almost down to my butt. I know you're thinking to yourself, was there enough material to cover things? Well, um…yes, or I wouldn't have worn it.

I would always go down to the village pool on my days off. The beach was never the same for me after prom and that night with Alia, and the smell of the lake in the thick of summer makes me retch to this day. I was an excellent diver, and unfortunately, I hadn't taken into consideration the style of the new suit.

Diary Of A Middle-Aged Mermaid

I came out of the ladies' locker room with a towel wrapped around my neck. My flip flops were flipping and flopping noisily, and my big movie star sunglasses were propped on my nose. I held my head high and strutted my stuff as I walked by the pool regulars in my new getup.

The men looked at me in...appreciation? Yeah, I'll call it that, and the women just gave me a look like they'd wished I'd crawl under a rock and disappear. I had what I thought was a pretty okay looking body at that time. I had been shedding off some of the donuts by working like a fiend, and I felt like I was looking sexy in that suit. My curves were where they needed to be, a few extra, but as far as I was concerned, in that suit, I was a damn fine-looking mermaid, if I do say so myself.

I shook out my towel and spread it on the lounge chair, set my glasses and bag aside, and rubbed suntan oil on myself. I was smelling of Hawaii and coconuts and shiny all over. I flung my shoulder-length hair back and tied it in a cute ponytail then proceeded to the diving board like I had done a thousand times before. I was looking good, I felt good, and it showed in my attitude.

The lifeguard watched as I chose the highest board out of the three the pool offered. Ten steps up, and I was two stories high and staring at the big blue concrete sea below me. My audience was watching with bated breath as they lounged in their chairs, and I walked to the edge like an Olympic star. One bounce, two bounce, stop, checking the tension of the board. You didn't want to have to correct mid-air or end up doing a belly flop.

I walked back to the edge of the board to begin my grandest feat. Higher and higher I bounced. With each touch down on the edge of the thin board, my arms were moving outward and with a simple elegance. I was arcing like a bird ready to take flight. As I gained more height, I lifted off. I was poised on the air like a beautiful swan, turning my body into position for the perfect dive. I hit the water with barely a splash. It was almost a ten, had it been a rated dive, and damn, I was feeling good. Feel free to cue up the Michael Buble song here, if you so desire.

I touched down on the bottom of the pool and pushed upwards. Springing through the water, I inhaled the warm air, swam over to the edge, and then began climbing up the side stairs next to the lifeguard to exit the pool. With a shock, I look down and realized that the strings holding my lovely suit on were now broken. They flowed around me like red and white candy-striped water snakes.

I've now gone and outdone Janet Jackson for wardrobe malfunction of the year. I'm trying to cover my breasts; the suit is sopping wet and began growing heavier. It was edging downward from the weight of the water. My pubic hair is flowing out of the high cut front like wild brown overgrown sea grass, and no one is jumping up and offering to bring me a towel to cover myself. I only have two hands to block the view from intrigued souls who gawked at me, and my face is lit up with the brightest shades of sunburn and embarrassment red combined.

I walked over to my towel looking like a child that has to pee. My legs were held clenched tight to hold the lower half of the suit somewhat in place, and my hands are coving the girls as if they're trying to escape from Alcatraz.

The lifeguard finally blows his whistle and diverts attention, while I grab my towel and wrap it tightly around my defective suit. I slink into the ladies' room, change into my shorts and tank top, and deposit that forty-dollar suit right into the garbage can. It lay there, such a sad looking thing, a sopping-wet striped lump beside a piss warm half-full Pepsi bottle and the remnants of sandwiches that were swarming in flies. I decided that, from that point on, there would be no more fancy suits for me, just the variety that are meant for actual swimming, not for exhibition of girl parts or centerfold spreads in *Cosmopolitan*.

Chapter Seven

Finding treasure, and with a little luck, a Pearl.

1986

I worked at Carl's Catch for a few years. If you worked at a restaurant anywhere near the lake in Buffalo, winter could be difficult. Life slowed down then, and I think, as Carl got up there in years, he wanted to spend more time fishing. To do that much fishing, it would be best to move to where he could do it all the time…in the sun, ALL the time. Buffalo wasn't going to benefit him in full-time sunny hooking of finned fishies, so he threw a lavish Christmas party and told us that he was going to be retiring and selling the joint. His hundred dollar present to each employee wasn't enough to cheer us up. Merry Christmas, suckers, see ya.

The restaurant was set to be sold. If new owners were found, Carl said, there was a chance that we could be picked up for employment. I shook my head, thinking to myself, who the heck buys a restaurant on a cliff, on a lake, in the sub-zero of winter? There were many restaurants around the area and work was easy enough to be found, but it was sad to realize that this stage of my life was coming to an end. We wished him well, and he shut the doors after the New Year's Eve celebrations wound down. New Years was always a huge money maker, and why close before collecting on the last big hurrah? Carl was a greedy guy that way, but it gave us an extra week and a half of work.

Carl moved to some ritzy beach in Florida, and the restaurant floundered; weather-beaten, it grew unsightly and remained unsold. The cliff it was on was eroding, and no one wanted to take the chance and bite the bullet on the old fixer-upper. I thought about it years later. I imagined serving up some fancy cheesecake as the whole building slid off the cliff, crashing down into the lake, killing us all. I'm glad those days are well behind me. They finally ended up tearing it down a few years later, and now there's a nice little park area with some benches where people can watch the sunset.

I'm not sure where the rats went. Did I mention that Carl's had been infested with rats? They lived in the basement. They came up from the beach, and they could be seen running through the kitchen occasionally. I got drunk one night at a late-night soirée, and I crashed out in the banquet room rather than drive home drunk. I woke up at one point, and I swore that I could hear them. They were moving around in the dark, scurrying along the wall. By that time, I felt sober enough to get behind the wheel instead of getting rabies shots in my belly if one of the little nasties bit me. Other than that, they never bothered me.

Once, a fuzzy brown rat did land on one of those sticky pads the exterminator set out to catch it. I'll be damned if that thing didn't use the paper like a pogo stick and bounce its way through the kitchen and out to the dining area. We caught it in a pan before a customer saw it, but it was a close call. We named him Simon and put him down on the beach to make his way from there. I'm not sure where Simon ended up, but I couldn't bring myself to deal him the final blow. I hope he freed himself and made his way down the beach to the other fish house.

I was now an unemployed twenty-something woman. As life tends to do, in the strangest of ways, it throws some amazing people into your path when you most need it.

I was in the local drugstore. Mr. Andrews of the bath bead incident is long dead, and his store has been changed in to a fancy new one, a CVS or RiteAid, one of those. I'm in the "lady needs" aisle comparing the differences on the boxes of corks, and this crazy woman comes whipping around the corner and slams into me with her cart. Now I'm not small, so let's just say that I'm pretty easy to spot. Boom! That hard metal cart slices right into my leg. I go down in a big heaping lump like a rhino shot on safari. I'm rolling on the floor, grunting and crying. I'm grasping my leg, trying to stop the flow of blood, but it hurts like a bitch. The irony wasn't lost on me at the time that, here I am in an aisle of items created to staunch the flow of blood, but I won't open one up to help myself.

I guess there must have been a jagged edge on the cart, and it sliced through me near the top of my ankle. I'm bleeding all over the pretty carpet in the shiny new drug store, and the woman moves around her weapon, I mean the cart, and she sees my leg and starts freaking out. The manager comes running over to see what all the ruckus is about, and then he sees my leg, and I swear to God, he faints right then and there. He hits his head on the corner of the shelf, and now he's bleeding on the floor. Maybe it was the idea of a lawsuit from sharp implements exposed on their carts that caused him to keel over like that. Whatever, we were both pathetic looking now.

The aisle is beginning to look like a Mafia massacre. It's a blood bath in aisle 9. An employee peeks around the corner and says she's calling the police. Maybe she thought we had a fist fight or something. Hey, call us an ambulance, Chickie; the police aren't needed. She rushes off, and the woman who ran me down isn't quite sure what to do first. There are two bodies down and blood, lots of blood. My ankle hurts like the dickens, and I'm holding my tongue to keep myself from screaming at her.

The cart-wielding woman wore these really thick glasses, and she must have been half-blind. I try to stand up, and that foot is not working without an excruciating amount of pain accompanying it. The cops show up, and this woman is babbling to them about what she had done to me, and they finally call the emergency squad. They took me to the same clinic where the Alia incident occurred, and an x-ray and a multitude of stitches later, come to find out my ankle is broken and my tendon is cut slightly. Well, cast me up and call me screwed. I know that I can't work with a broken ankle. Being a waitress is a fast-paced job, and the crutches on greasy floors are not a good idea. It's a restaurant's worst fear when a customer comes in on them, and you'll notice more carpets strategically placed to insure against a lawsuit. I'm wondering to myself, what the hell do I do now? I need to work, and I now need to reassess my options.

When I'm finally released, four hours, a cast, and a shiny set of crutches later, I find the woman who hit me out in the waiting room. She starts crying when she sees me and offers to give me a ride home. There's no one else, and my car is back at the drug store, so I accept. I hobble out to her car, trying to get the hang of the sticks under my pits, and she opens the door to this big old Cadillac. I'm impressed. I don't know how she could see to drive, and if I wasn't on a pain killer that was finally kicking in, I may have had the thought that, with her cart maneuvering skills, perhaps she's not the best option for a safe ride in a thirty-five-hundred-pound car, especially with her behind the wheel. Her name was Pearl, and she turned out to be a very nice lady, who would ultimately turn my life in a new direction.

Pearl told me that she was married to a doctor and that she helped him out in the office. She didn't need to work; she just liked helping people and keeping busy. I think I laughed out loud when she told me that. I was thinking that she likes to make patients for her husband's business, ramming them with carts and breaking bones while looking all innocent. It must have been the drugs, I swear, but that's what I was thinking.

She asked me what I did for a living, and now I'm laughing harder. I told her I was currently job hunting and that now I'm screwed. She began crying again. She pulled to the side of the road and parked the car. There was a big box of Kleenex wedged between the seats, and she grabbed one and blew her nose. It sounded like a squeaky trumpet, and I started laughing again.

Those drugs were pretty good. She turned and stared at me, and I stopped laughing. The look on her face made me want to cry.

"I'm going to give you a job. You can come and work in the office. I'll teach you what you need to know. I'll pay you twelve dollars an hour and time and a half for overtime. You can sit; you won't have to stand. Would you want to come work for me?"

Now keep in mind, as a waitress, I had been making $2.01 an hour plus tips (which had to be split with the cook and dishwasher). I think I sat there for a minute with my mouth on the floor as my pea-brain processed what she was saying. Then I smiled. I was feeling like things were getting brighter. I told her yes, and she started crying again.

"You're going to enjoy it, I think. I don't know you, but you seem to be an educated young lady, and the work isn't very hard. You'll be learning the insurance codes for billing, and I think you'll pick it up easily enough. I'm glad you said yes. I feel horrible about what happened, and we were looking for help for the office, so I guess we will help each other. Do you have a few minutes to come with me to the office? This way you can see it and decide if you still would like to work with us. I'm the office manager, and we have a lot of patients, so work is always booming. If you don't feel up to it though, I understand."

I told her it would be fine, and I was now getting excited about the prospect of a real adult job. I wouldn't be coming home smelling like fried foods, and best of all, my clothes wouldn't be all scummy and greasy at the end of the day.

My brain switched gears on me, and I started getting worried. I wasn't sure if I had proper clothing that would be acceptable wear for an office job. I told her my concerns, and she said she'd give me an advance to pick up what I needed. I leaned my head back and watched as she maneuvered this big boat of a car down the side streets, and then she pulled up in front of a small building at the end of the street. It had a cement porch with a metal ramp that would enable wheelchair bound patients access to the door. It was strange, trying to go up a slope on the crutches and drugged up on pain-killers, but I managed it without falling backwards and tumbling down the thing.

The office was very bright and looked like it had a recent coat of paint. It was orderly, and it smelled nice and clean. I met her husband, Dave. Dr. Dave was a kindly gentleman who had a bright sparkle to his eyes. He laughed a lot, it was a nice light sound, and it seemed like a very happy place. I looked at Pearl and said yes, definitely yes, to the job. She told me I wouldn't have to start working for a week or until the pain edged off a bit on the broken ankle.

She went in the office and wrote me out a check for $150 for clothing and told me I didn't have to pay it back, that it was the least she could do after injuring me. I tucked the check in my purse and then met the other office worker. She was a middle-aged heavy-set woman named Helen and seemed very nice.

So, Pearl and I got back in the car, and she drove me home. She had made arrangements to get my car back to me while we were at the office, and I had given her the key so she could give it to the towing company, and then she followed me inside to make sure that I had everything I needed.

Harmony wasn't home yet. She was working down at an ice-cream stand, and yes, people do eat a lot of ice cream in Buffalo, even in the thick of winter, believe it or not. She wouldn't be back for hours. Pearl had me go sit in the La-Z-Boy, and she poured me a glass of lemonade before she left. I just wanted to sleep. The drug was really kicking in and now making me groggy. I thanked her and, at some point, drifted off. I remember dreaming that I was swimming in the ocean, doing mermaid things with my legs intact, and I remember feeling happy for the first time in ages.

Seven days later, I'm out of drugs and the happy feeling has dissipated. Now I was feeling it. It was a Saturday, and I didn't start work until Monday. Pearl was checking in daily, and this morning she was coming over to take me clothes shopping. She knocked on the door and walked in carrying a basket of homemade organic muffins, both blueberry and raspberry, with chocolate bits in them. She sat them on the counter, and I grabbed my purse, and we hopped into the Cadillac. Its name was Bruce the Beast, my name for it, not hers.

We pulled up to a consignment shop, and I looked at the clothes in the window. Not exactly my style, I thought to myself, and these are things I would never have worn had I been paying. Pearl knew the owner and said we'd start out there. We walked into the store. The scent of pricy perfume filled the air, and I walked down through the racks and touched the material. They were so soft, and I could tell they were high-quality fabrics. I'm picturing myself at this point with one hell of a dry-cleaning bill, and I think Pearl figured it out as I looked at the care tags inside the clothes. She guided me towards more easy-care items, to which I was thankful. I let her pull a couple of outfits together that she liked for me. I watched everything that she chose, hoping to get my thunder thighs and wide hips squeezed into the straight clinging skirts. I walked into the dressing room filled with dread.

I never try clothes on in a store. In some stupid class in high school, we watched a movie on shoplifting, and they showed how security people were watching cameras that were set up behind those big-assed mirrors that were in each dressing stall. Nope, no, and thank you, but definitely no. I'd rather return something that didn't fit than have anyone watching me change. I don't know if it's true about those cameras, and if it's not, then I think that it is a really shitty way to build paranoia in unsuspecting teens.

So now I have to strip down. I was happy that I had worn my best bra and panties, and Pearl is good; she nailed it on the sizes, and I didn't think that I looked too bad. I felt kind of grown up. I was all gussied up for a real job, and with Pearl picking out the clothes, I knew that they'd be sufficient for the office.

She kept bringing me outfits, and by the time I was done, I knew I'd blown way past the $150 that she had given me. I picked out the two outfits I liked the best, and she told me no, I was taking all of them. The bill tallied up to almost four hundred dollars, and I blanched as the cheery-faced sales clerk said it aloud. I could see her mind churning at the commission she was going to make, and I told Pearl it was too much. She waved me away, paid it all with a credit card, and wished me a Happy Birthday, which wasn't for another five months, mind you. That woman sure knew how to spark the gratitude tears. She hugged me tight and told me that it was a gift.

61

I think Pearl was one of the kindest people I've ever met. I wished at that minute that she would have been my mother, then felt guilty for even thinking it, and I learned to appreciate her as a substitute mom after that. So, a slew of bags later, we head out for lunch.

I like pizza, so Pearl drove me to my favorite place, Uno's Pizzeria, and we walked in to find a seat. It was after lunch, so I was able to find a booth that had enough room for my leg to stretch out fully without being hit by someone walking by. We looked over the menu, but I always got the same thing every time I went, which was weekly. I ordered a personal pizza with double cheese and pepperoni. They had the best kind of pepperoni, the kind that, when cooked right, the edges would curl up, and they turned that perfect shade of almost burnt. Pearl, who of course is a tiny thing, ordered a chicken Caesar salad.

She told me about her life while we waited for the food. She had worked two jobs to put Dr. Dave through med school, and they had one son. He was a late life baby, a "surprise," she said with a laugh. He was in college and finishing up his last year of med school. A chip off the old block, she muttered cheerfully, and I could see the love for him light up her face when she talked about him. His name was Alec, and he was in Georgetown. He was specializing in Neurology. She was proud of who he had become, she said, and she pulled out her wallet and showed me a picture of him. He was hot, hotter than hot. She saw the look on my face and chuckled.

"All the ladies love Alec, but he was always a little odd around girls. He was more involved in anything related to science and just never made the time for any one special girl. I hope to get grandkids at some point, but until he's ready, I suppose I'll just have to wait." I nodded, and the waitress came over with our food. I felt almost guilty as I ate my big cheesy slice with a fork and knife while Pearl picked daintily on her healthy salad.

I know I'm fat, and I always think that people are judging me. I think it's because I judge myself, so then I think that everyone sees me as I see me. Pearl didn't even bat an eyelash when I dove into my pizza like a starving woman. It's how I always ate my pizza. Doesn't everyone? But she asked if she could have a bite, so I cut her a chunk and slid it over to the edge of her salad plate. She chewed it thoughtfully and smiled.

"This is heaven. I can see why you like it so much," and then she went back to her greens. I looked at her clothes, which were refined and very tasteful. She looked like she didn't have an ounce of fat on her. I guessed her to be around 60, and I asked her. She swallowed before answering then told me she was 63. I suppose if I cared, I too would eat a salad, but comfort food was just that, my comfort. It had been since my mother died, and when I was down in the dumps, or bored, or whatever excuse I could muster, I ate. It always worked, so why change now? But looking at Pearl, I realized I wanted more for myself. I wanted to look good in my clothes. I wanted that perfect essence that she had. I don't know what you'd call it, energy? Yes, I wanted, I craved to possess that soul charging happy energy. When Pearl walked in a room, she exuded this beauty, straight from the inside, and I longed to have just a teensy tiny piece of it.

Then she asked the question I never quite know how to answer.

"What did you aspire to become? What did you want to be when you were a little girl?"

I stopped chewing as the words came from her mouth and her eyes gave such a compassionate look. I could tell that she really cared about how I would answer, and I calmly stated, "a mermaid." I thought she'd laugh then, but she nodded and smiled brightly.

"Well, that's a grand idea. I think you'd be a beautiful mermaid. So, why didn't you become one?" and I really had to stop and think about that.

"I think you have to be born with the outfit, and now I wouldn't be able to get my big butt into one. I hear they have a side show down in Florida where women do dress up like mermaids. They swim in this big pool of green water, and they're sucking off of air hoses and doing tricks while leering men and families watch them through a big glass window beneath them. It's kind of like they're in a jumbo-sized aquarium. I don't want to do that. I just like the idea of being a strong and beautiful woman, swimming far and wide, no troubles or cares, no responsibility. I know, it's stupid, but when I was a girl, that's what I wanted, and I still do, I suppose."

Pearl continued eating her salad and nodding at me, and then she put down her fork and reached across the table and took my hand in hers.

"Being a mermaid, as I sit here and think about it, is a state of mind. A strong woman who knows what she wants and isn't afraid to ask for it. Beauty comes from within, and I don't think it's about being a supermodel with fins; it's just a belief in yourself that shines through. That to me is a mermaid. I think you're a lovely one, and that's my opinion, for what it's worth."

I thought about what she said and remembered back to when I had courage with the pharmacist about the bath beads, the way it felt to stand up for my convictions, a super girl with an imaginary cape. I wondered whatever happened to that girl. I vowed that, when I got home, I was going to make a list of my goals and work towards being a better me.

It was going to start here and now. I asked the waitress to bring me a box for the rest of the pizza, when normally I would have eaten the whole thing and not thought twice about it. I asked Pearl if we could stop by the stationery store. I needed to get myself a pretty book to fill up with my dreams and goals, and she said that it would be no problem.

We left the restaurant a short time later, and I went into the store, found the right aisle, and perused the books. They were big beautiful blank books, and I realized that, starting today, I was going to treat life like that big blank book. Emptiness waiting to be filled with wishes, hopes, and dreams. I finally settled on one with a beautiful, can you believe it, mermaid on the cover. She smiled coyly, her long brown hair was draped around her breasts like a cloak, and it had sparkly jewels surrounding her. Step one was now accomplished, and so many more to go.

Pearl dropped me off and helped me in with my packages. She said goodbye and that she'd see me on Monday then left.

I turned on the tv and channel surfed and didn't see much of anything, until an infomercial came on for a diet aid called Metabolife 356. It looked promising, and I knew I needed some major help. Being on crutches wasn't going to allow me to lose the weight easily, and working full time wouldn't help either, especially sitting. If I couldn't lose it as a waitress, I was now going to need a miracle.

I opened up my new goal book and filled in the first entry, starting weight...and then I got really scared. I hadn't stepped on a scale in at least a year or longer, more towards the end of longer, if I'm being truthful. I heaved myself up and onto the crutches then stumbled off towards the bathroom. I picked up a towel with my toes and swiped away the dust on the scale, in my mind fearing that any particulate would add an extra pound or something. I then closed my eyes and stepped on the torture device. The spinner flew back and forth like a carnival game before finally coming to rest on 250 pounds. I took a deep breath and exhaled, hoping to shave anything off the horrid truth, but was left with a little wiggle of the spinner, before it planted its evil ass back on 250.

I cried like a baby then. "What the fuck? What have I done," I said to the walls, and I stepped off the scale and kicked it across the room, unfortunately using the foot with the cast.

"Jesus H. Christ," I screamed, the pain flowing through me like an army of fire ants running up my leg. I sat down on the toilet and cried some more, staring at the scale and wishing it would just disappear. It didn't happen. I got back up and looked at myself in the mirror.

"It's now or never, girl. Time to get real and face the music." I wiped the gobs of snot off my face and looked at myself in the mirror.

"When did I get two chins?" the little voice in my head was asking, and then it began answering me in earnest; pizza, bacon, chips, and everything else I had shoveled into my pie-hole is what had happened. Drinking the booze didn't help much either, I realize. But what to do about it now?

I hobbled back into the living room, grabbed my book, and watched the before and after images of the fat to skinny people on the tv. They were all so happy and grinning at me. I picked up the phone and dialed the blinking number that demanded I call now before it was too late.

The nice lady from India, or wherever the hell she was talking to me from, took my information and told me that for an extra ten dollars I could get it shipped in two days. Of course, I said yes.

I made a note in the mermaid book about this wonder drug and pondered what should come next. My mind was visualizing my body after a month on this "amazing" new wonder pill, and I smiled. I could be a mermaid, I could be happy, and I could be healthy too.

Chapter Eight

A mermaid gets sweaty... rising up, one fin at a time.

Auntie Kate,

I'm a fat slob, and now I know it. But what to do about it? First things first, stop saying negative shit about myself. I know, don't remind me. Even self-help books have some bits of wisdom in them sometimes, and that's a nugget I'm keeping.

Patience was never a virtue for me, and I realize that it's going to take a shit-ton of willpower, not to mention time, but I'm determined now. I bought the new book with a mermaid on the cover, and I'm filling it with important things, not to say that you're not important. It's like having two lovers, not that I have any idea what that's like, but you get my emotions, and it gets my game plan.

I need to change. I realize that, if I ever want to hit my goals, I'm going to have to start now. Pearl is amazing and she is so wise. She says so much without saying much at all. It has been well over two years since mom's been gone, and Alia, who never really had a chance, died, and I know I want more out of this life than what I'm settling for.

I had asked Harmony that night, when she got home from work, when I had become so obese. She looked at me with some apprehension, and I think she was afraid to say anything. She just figured I knew, so why bring it up and make me feel bad?

She sat the bag down that held a big butter-pecan milkshake in it that was meant for me. I looked at it and started crying. She took it into the kitchen and dumped it down the garbage disposal. She was going to be graduating that year, and she's kind of where I was back then, skinny as a rail and with her whole life ahead of her. I asked her not to bring me any more milkshakes home from work or any ice cream. She was sweet though and asked if I can eat sugar-free. I told her I'd have to look into it, but why open up that can of worms…

My pills would be here the next day, and I hoped they'd help. Pearl was going to take me food shopping, and I asked her for help in making wiser eating choices. She hugged me so hard and said of course, so I've got her and Harmony in my corner. She bought me a cookbook on eating healthy, and I'm not a great cook, but I looked at some of the recipes that even I, Miss Mermaid floundering in a kitchen, could make. I also found some old free weights out in the garage and started using them religiously. I had a plan, even with the broken ankle. At least it's something. I can do leg lifts on the floor and sit ups with my leg on a pillow. I may look silly, I thought, but it had to be done.

I hate sweating, so Harmony brought me a big fan into the living room, and I could use that to stave off the endless perspiration. Work started the next day, too, and thank God I bought, or I should say, Pearl bought the skirts. Pants with this cast were out of the question, unless they're harem pants, and God knows I didn't need to look any larger. Pearl most likely had figured that out too. I told you that she was wise.

Dinner that night was a big salad. I wasn't thrilled or even remotely excited. I was angry. I want to cry and rage against whatever happened to me along the way, but I realized that blame was just shifting things away from truth. I'm being honest with myself, even if it kills me. So, wish me luck.

I did fifteen leg lifts, and I know that these mermaid legs will get there someday, but damn, my muscles hurt. I had only managed five sit-ups, and I hoped each night that I could add more. I was nervous about the new job. I'd never done that kind of work before, so I hoped I would do all right. I know, Dest; just be positive. Okay, I will be amazing tomorrow, is that better? I thought so. I made a lot of updates to that mermaid goal book about what I wanted and how I planned on executing my goals. Sorry, I guess I don't have much to say today. Tomorrow, I promise I'll tell you all about it.

I loved my new job. Everyone was so nice, and they bought me lunch, a big salad that was pretty fancy. Pearl performed wonders with training me at work and encouraging me, and Helen was pretty nice, too. I remember seeing her looking at me sometimes in a certain way. I don't know if it was out of pity or jealousy, but I wasn't going to let it bother me. This is a new Destiny, and I'm standing up for myself, with crutches, but almost standing, right? When I get home every evening, I'll do my exercises, and the pills came. They're supposed to fill you up so that you eat less. I crossed my fingers and toes that they would work.

Kate,

So, I started the pills a half an hour before dinner. I had another salad with some grilled chicken boobs, and I swore that I'd be turning into a rabbit before I was through. The pills didn't bother my stomach, and I had to drink a big glass of water with them, but I was full when I finished. Let's see if it holds out through my normal snack time tonight. If they do, then I think they will be working. But if I'm mowing down an entire bag of salt and vinegar chips and some pizza, I'm throwing them in the garbage.

I put a big sheet of paper up on the wall in the bathroom, and I will weigh myself every day. I also put a centerfold of a model from an old *Sports Illustrated* swimsuit issue up beside it to encourage me. I know, I'm never going to be supermodel material, but I know someday, beneath all the jelly rolls, there lurked a mermaid in waiting. I did read something interesting on mermaids, and I'm not sure whether I agree or believe it. I think any fool can write what they want in Wikipedia; maybe it is fake news, you can be the judge, but what I found out was this:

"Historical accounts of mermaids, such as those reported by Christopher Columbus during his exploration of the Caribbean, may have been inspired by manatees and similar aquatic mammals. While there is no evidence that mermaids exist outside folklore, reports of mermaid sightings continue to the present day."

Have you ever seen a manatee? I think they're something like twenty-five hundred pounds or so; they are HUGE! Maybe I already am a mermaid and just didn't know it. I realize that curvaceous Rubenesque women were popular back then, but my God, really? I can't let it dissuade me from losing weight. I will make no excuses. I will be a wonderful sexy mermaid. Watch and see. I've got to go. I'm trying to limit my free time to working out instead of sitting on my ass and talking to you, but you do serve an important part in my life. Don't worry. I won't forget you, my paper friend. Got to run, Kate. Will talk soon.

Don't be angry with me, but it seems I've forgotten you again. It has been six months, and things are going great. The pills are working, and it's like a miracle has happened. I've lost fifty-one pounds so far, and I finally hit 199 on the scale. I'm halfway to the goal, baby, and damn, it feels good. The cast has been gone for a little while now, and work is going great. I'm making good money, and believe it or not, I finally met someone, meaning a guy someone. He's really nice, super cute, and I think he likes me too. I'm of course nervous as a cat in a room full of coyotes, but maybe that's why I remembered you. You were always good to talk to when I'm feeling this way. I don't want to go backwards and start eating my way through everything in sight out of fear and anxiety. Keep me calm, Kate. I know you can do it.

So, about the new man. His name is Alec, and he's the son of Pearl and Dr. Dave. He just finished grad school and came back home to visit. When he walked into the office, my eyes just about fell out of my head. I've never seen a more perfect man in my life. He's really tall and has this beautiful dirty-blonde wavy hair. He's muscular and that butt of his, whew, maybe I shouldn't go there. It's been so long since I've even had any interest in a man, and here walks in this Adonis. The only thing I could think of when I saw him was what an absolutely beautiful man he was. He was funny, too. When he talks to you, he looks you square in the eyes, as if he's really interested in what you have to say, which with me, isn't much at all. I was too tongue-tied.

Pearl and Dave are throwing him a welcome home party tomorrow night, and I'm invited. I'm not sure what I should buy him as a gift, but I'll ask Pearl. She'll know what he'd like. Pearl told me he was kind of socially awkward when he was younger, but he didn't seem that way to me at all. I should know; I'm the queen of socially awkward after all. I'm going to go work out, as I won't get any time in tomorrow after work, so double duty on the squats jumps. Got to tone up that ass, which is shrinking by the way. I guess things are looking up, and I'm getting kind of excited now. Thanks Kate, you always know how to make me feel better.

Aunt Kate,

I don't know why I keep ignoring you. I guess I've just been pretty busy. It's been two more months now, and I had to go back to see where I left off with you. The party was great. I got Alec a mug engraved with Dr. Alec on it. He really liked it. He likes beer, the good stuff, so I know he's been getting use out of it. He works at the hospital. He had the chance to leave town and move down south, but they made him an offer he couldn't refuse, and after the party, he asked me out. Yes, moi, Fatty McMermaid…oh, sorry, I'm being a negative Nelly again.

I've lost twenty more pounds, and my energy has been through the roof. I jog now, too. I joined the local swimming pool, so when I'm not working, I'm working out. I am determined to hit my goal, even if it kills me. On a sad note, the FDA went to town on the pill company and whatever was in it, ephedra or something like that. Apparently, it was causing heart attacks in people and killed some, too. They made them pull out that particular ingredient. The bad part is that the new stuff doesn't work nearly as well as the old stuff. So, I'm having to get creative and really buckle down to toe the line.

I bought a pair of roller blades. Can you believe it? Can you see me on rollerblades? The old Destiny wouldn't have even attempted it. Picture a big old happy walrus moving down the street on wheels; hit one bump and my girls would fly up and take my head off. But the new me is pretty good at it, and it's a great cardio workout, just in case those pills caused any damage.

Alec and I have become an item since we last spoke. He works a ton, and I don't get to see him very often. We go out to dinner and to the movies when he's free, which isn't often. I really like him a lot, and he's encouraging me when it comes to losing the weight. He never saw me back when I was huge and at my heaviest, but he knows I'm being diligent on eating. He's a vegan, so it works out well. He's found all the great restaurants to go to, and it's helping. I don't remember the last time I binged on junk food, and I haven't had a donut, yes, no donuts, since I started the job at Dr. Dave's.

Alec bought a house in the city. It's on Delaware over by the zoo, and it's in a good part of Buffalo. It's pretty close to the hospital. I've been spending some nights there when I can.

Harmony left for college, so it's just me at the house. I've turned the living room into the workout room, and when I get in from work, I chug a green smoothie and get to it. I crank the tunes and haven't gotten any complaints from the neighbors yet, so that's good. Maybe they just really like disco. I mean, who doesn't, right?

Chapter Nine

A mermaid looks back, why? To look forward, of course.

I hit the three-year anniversary of my mom's death. I hadn't thought of it much at all; maybe I just didn't want to. We were always close but not too close. Before she died, she was working two jobs, so I never got to see her much in my teen years. I think she'd be proud of me, of the weight I've lost and of who I'm becoming.

I never told you about Dad because there's not much to say about him. He left when I was 10, apparently not enamored with his life. The prick took off out of state with some slut that he worked with. She was at least fifteen years younger than him, too. Mom never said much about him after that, and he never calls, and I don't call him either. He owed a ton of child support but played the unemployment card to get out of it. That's why Mom worked so much. I heard he had another kid too, so I suppose I have a step sibling out there somewhere, but honestly, I don't really care.

I think I'll go down and put some flowers on her grave. I don't go there very often, and I did come to a decision because of the thought of visiting graves and such. If I ever die, I want to be cremated and my remains scattered out on the ocean waves. Maybe the Gulf of Mexico, I hear it's beautiful there. I think it would be just the perfect final place for a mermaid to rest after a long weary life.

Things are going hot and heavy with Alec. We've been discussing where we want to head in this relationship, and I think we both pretty much agree. I've never met anyone like him before, and I'm not going to be getting any younger. I want to have kids before I'm too old to enjoy them. Alec does too. He's amazing in bed, and we just click like we were meant for each other. I thought about it the other day; had Pearl not broken my ankle and taken pity on me, I'd have never met her or Alec.

Work is great, and I've been bumped up to office manager, too. Pearl wants to do more behind the scenes work, and she's been looking tired lately. I think something's up, but I'm not going to ask her. If something is amiss, I'm sure she'd say something. Alec says she looks fine, but he hasn't been around her for years, with school, so how would he know? I've just got my super sense elevated. I'll keep my eyes open.

I've lost another ten pounds, and I'm almost there. Twenty more to go and boom! I'll be the most smoking hot mermaid you've ever seen. Oh, and Alec put an addition on his house, adding an indoor in-ground pool. It's heated, and he is adding a hot tub in the corner of the room, too. I'm helping him redecorate the interior. I never knew I had such a flair for color, but he's loving the choices I make, and he's paying for it all, of course. Carte blanche is my favorite when it comes to decorating someone else's house. So, I guess you could say things are going well for me finally.

Aunt Kate,

So it's another happy birthday to me. Come on, sing along. Alec proposed last night. YAY! He took me down to the lake to watch the sunset, and we had a couple of beers. I only had a half of one, in case you were wondering, because there are too many carbs in the stuff he likes. I was not expecting it, let's just say, but I said yes. He's been working so much, and maybe by getting married and living together, we may be able to see more of each other. He is in neurosurgery. I'm not sure if I told you that or not, but he makes excellent money. He enjoys it, and he's been able to knock off a lot of his student loan with the extra work he's been doing. I'm still at Dr. Dave's, and things are pretty much day to day there. Pearl is looking very tired lately, and I heard Alec talking to Dr. Dave about her. They saw me standing outside the office and politely closed the door, so I'll have to ask him later, if he'll tell me.

So, we haven't set a date yet, but we have all the time in the world. It's July. I just realized I haven't been putting dates in you, but that's okay; it is really not that important. Maybe a spring wedding, the possibilities are endless.

Aunt Kate,

Pearl has lung cancer, stage 4. The woman never smoked a cigarette in her life, and she gets this. It sucks. She doesn't deserve this, and I'm so angry and sad all at the same time. Alec told me tonight that he wants to do an easy wedding somewhere in a park or on the beach. I opted for the beach, weather permitting. He's worried that she's not going to make it and wants her there on our big day. How could I not say yes? Two weeks from now, I will say I do. I've got to go get a dress and take care of the details. We're just going to go out for a nice dinner afterwards. I had all these dreams of a big fancy wedding, but in the big picture of things, it's important to us both to have Pearl in attendance. She was so excited to hear the news. Maybe that's why he told me what was wrong with her. I'm going to be family after all, and that made it okay.

I found my dress today. It was at Macy's, and it's beautiful and a flowing style white cotton and is tea length. It's light enough, which will help, because it's going to be hot on Saturday. Who would have thought 94 degrees in Buffalo in July? It just never happens. I got my hair frosted with blonde highlights, which made me look like a real mermaid. My dress size is down to a twelve now, and they only had one left. I lucked out there, I guess.

So, I ordered a bouquet of white and purple flowers for myself and a small one for Pearl. She and Dave are standing up for us because of the time crunch, and Alec didn't have time to get any of his buddies in from college, and I didn't want to pull Harmony away from her schooling for a quickie wedding. She's taking summer classes and working for the university. She's so happy for me, and we are having it filmed so that we can show everyone that we really did go through with it.

Pearl is fading fast, and I'm going to be so sad when she's gone. She and Dave sat me down and explained that the office will still go on as usual. Dr. Dave isn't retiring any time soon, but he will take off a few weeks when she passes. I've got a good bank account going, and I help Harmony out with some of her school fees, but Alec is in a good enough position to cover us both.

Cancer sucks. Did I tell you that already? I don't know what's worse. The way Mom died was hard; we had no chance to say goodbye, and now with Pearl, you've got the time, but you feel so damn helpless. I know, we all go sometime, but when it's right in your face like that, well it just makes it so much harder to deal with. Alec has been a rock for us all, and I'm so thankful for him for that. I am blessed, Kate. I really am.

Dear Kate,

We got married down at a small area on the beach that normally wasn't too populated. Thank God, it didn't smell like dead fish. Everybody and their brother was down there trying to cool off in the heat. We had a few people watching the ceremony, and they clapped when it was over, which I thought made it a little more festive. We made it as short as we could because Pearl was in a wheelchair and was fading like a daisy without water. We kissed quickly and made our way to the restaurant.

Pearl picked at her meal, not much of an appetite left anymore, and we both realized that it wouldn't be very much longer for her. She did try to stay as long as she could, but Dave drove her home after about forty-five minutes. Alec and I sat there quietly after they left. I just wanted to cry. What should have been one of the happiest days of my life had just become another one of the saddest. I picked at my filet mignon as he picked at his eggplant and pasta. They brought us out a small cake for our special day, and we held the knife and cut through it as I cried. Neither one of us wanted any of it, so they were kind enough to box it up to go. We got home, and we were both drained. We decided to hold off on consummating our marriage until the next day when we were more in the right frame of mind.

Dear Kate,

Pearl died the day after our wedding. Dr. Dave said that she slipped away in her sleep. She had been on morphine for pain, and he kissed her goodnight like he had always done. When he went in the next morning, she was gone. I'm so sad. I loved her so much, and I'm happy now that we decided to do the impromptu wedding on the beach. She was there to see her son get married, and I really believed that she loved me too. They are burying her in a mausoleum that holds some of their other family members.

The service was mobbed, so many of Dr. Dave's patients were there, and we ran out of chairs. It was standing room only at the church, which goes to show how much she was really loved by all. Alec took it well. His roommate, Brett, from college came, and he stayed with us. He's a doctor too, but he works down in Florida. He and Alec would stay up late at night, and I think by having his friend there, it helped him to deal with Pearl's passing easier. Brett is funny like Alec, but much more psychologically in-depth. He loves to pick your brain about things, and he has an odd way of twisting around what you say. I'm not sure if I liked that, but it didn't cause any harm; just made you think outside the box and in different ways. Life went on like always. The office reopened two weeks later, and now I've got mine and Pearl's workload. I'm not getting many workouts in, but I'm not ballooning out either.

Alec and I finally got around to the sex thing, making the marriage official, and it was nice. He was gentle and kind, and I wondered if I would have dated sooner if I had met someone like him way back then. No sense in wondering, I suppose, and as long as he's happy, I'm happy.

Dr. Dave is letting me hire an office worker to help out with the load. I've got interviews lined up next week, so I'll be learning a new trick. Helen is still Helen, and after I was made office manager, the true colors came out in force. She tries to make life difficult, but she'll be quitting next year when she turns sixty-five, so I'm making the best of it until then. I refuse to put up with any shit from her, don't get me wrong, but when someone tries to sabotage your mood on a daily basis, something has got to give.

I spoke to her once after the job change-over, and she was seething, but she took it. It was either that or quit. She needed the job, and I needed her, too. If nothing else, I'll know what qualities to look for in the next one I hire. Life is all about learning, constant learning, and I'm swimming along and managing nicely. Oh, and five more pounds to go, squeal!

Chapter Ten

Swimming in the deep end, the Chilean Sea bass episode.

Aunt Kate,

Well, I finally managed to hit my goal. Life is better at work, and I hired a nice girl named Kate, believe it or not. She's very smart, and she put Helen in her place on the first day. She's a take-charge kind of girl. She's older than me by about twenty years, but she makes me laugh, and she's competent, which is the most important thing. Dr. Dave likes her too. I see them talking together, and I think there may be love in the air in the future. He's like a new person. He's happy again and back to being the lighthearted Dave that I first met.

Alec has been balls to the walls busy, and I never see much of him. He's been having to travel to take seminars for work. It seems like every month he's off to somewhere new. He would take me along, but with the office being so busy, there's no time to get away. I'd love to go see some new places, but he always brings me back a trinket from wherever he's been.

I've been trying to work out every day when I get home, and I actually succeed most of the time. I've been doing laps in the pool every morning just in case and no more pills. I don't need them anymore because I watch what I eat. I hate cooking for just myself with Alec constantly gone, so it seems to be a lot of salads again. Cutting carbs and sugars helps a lot, but sometimes I will have a glass of Merlot with dinner.

Alec has been talking about moving down south. He's tired of the cold and the snow. We have someone to plow the driveway and shovel the walk, we have the money to spend between both our salaries, but I'm not sure. I grew up here, and it has always been home to me. He knows Kate could easily take over responsibilities at work, and then I could live a life of leisure, married to a rich doctor. They offered him some good money down in Tampa. He's gone down and talked to them apparently, without telling me about it, which pissed me off. His buddy Brett works down there too, and he calls often and extolls the virtue of living next to a beautiful ocean.

"You could finally be the mermaid you've always dreamed of," he'd tell me, trying to sway me to his way of thinking, and I guess after a while, I could see it too. We put the house on the market, and it sold within a month. The housing market in Buffalo wasn't very good at the time, so maybe we just found the right person at the right time. Kate took over my job, and Dr. Dave sent us away with a big hug and some tears. The moving van came and took what we were taking down with us, which wasn't much. The furniture up north seems too clunky and dark, whereas the ocean houses down there are furnished with light and airy pieces.

Harmony was still off in school, and we hadn't decided what to do with our old house. She wasn't sure where she would settle after school, but she finally gave me the blessing to sell it, knowing that if she wanted to, she was always welcome at the new seaside home. That house took a bit longer to sell. It took almost a year and a half. It needed a lot of work, and I wasn't going to be around to do it. When it did sell, I took the money and put it away to help Harmony pay off her student loan debt.

So, we were now fresh new residents of Venice, Florida. Our house was out on the island, overlooking the Gulf of Mexico. It was the grandest house I had ever been in, and I was worried about whether we could afford it. Alec told me not to be concerned, what with the payment from the Buffalo house. I didn't have to work, and he was given a sizable bonus for signing on with the hospital, and he didn't even bitch about the commute every day. He told me he could stay with Brett if it was too far a drive after a long day, and I saw no problem with that.

I went out and did some furniture shopping, amazed at all the things out there. I couldn't decide, so I picked up some interior decorating magazines for ideas. I think, in the long run, I did pretty well, too. The only fly in the ointment of my life was that we'd been married for not quite two years now, and there were still no babies swimming in my blue womb. I began to wonder if he'd ever be around enough to work on it with me, 'cause it takes two, after all. He had a vacation coming up, and we decided to spend it together and work on it, one on one. No golf games, no entertaining, just spending it like we did in the old days. Dinner and movies and whatever else we wanted.

He surprised me by chartering a boat. It was more like a yacht, and I guess it belonged to a co-worker doctor friend. We had a captain and first mate and little interference. That first night, we had sex like rabbits. I had been paying attention to the monthly charts, and according to statistics, it was a good time to try. The second day was more like halfhearted rabbits, and then after that, we just hung out on deck, sunning and fishing and listening to tunes while we talked about his job.

The fishing was good, and the first mate would cook up whatever he caught, and by the end of the trip, I was pretty sick of fish. Alec, at some point, left the vegan lifestyle without ever mentioning it, and had begun to incorporate fish into his diet. I was good with it, and he seemed to relish fishing and the meals it provided. I just disliked the lack of information and changes in him. We'd always been able to talk; now I was always being surprised.

Three or four weeks after the fishing trip, we went out for a nice dinner. I think perhaps I had been whining a bit about never seeing him, so it was his way of pacifying me. It was a fancy place on the bay, and I watched as the sun set down into the blue green water. It was relaxing, and I even had a chance to play dress up, something I rarely did anymore. I was tan, the perfect weight finally, and life was sitting there before my fins like paradise. I think I was happy. I was happy. Alec ordered the lobster, and I got the Chilean sea bass. It was encrusted in macadamia nuts and drizzled with a raspberry balsamic glaze. It was to die for. I had never had that fish before, and I thought about it and laughed. I looked at Alec, and he was watching me, wondering what was so funny.

"I'm a mermaid, and here I sit eating my brethren. Isn't there something odd about that?" He found it funny and laughed too. I took a sip of my Pinot Grigio. Did I mention I had started drinking more often too? I looked at him. He had a new haircut, and for some reason, he just looked different to me. It was almost like I didn't know him anymore. He'd changed so much in the time since our marriage, and maybe it's just that I was the one changing. I don't know. I finished my wine and ordered another one. He asked me what was wrong, but I didn't know what to say.

We declined desert when the waiter swung by. He paid the bill, and we went home. When we got there, he said he had some work to do, so I stood there in the hallway in this big beautiful cold mansion and watched him walk away. I went into the kitchen and poured myself a drink, another Pinot, and I took it out onto the balcony that overlooked the water. I glanced up at his office. It was lit up brightly, and I saw that he was on the phone. I breathed in the balmy and humid night air and just felt so empty. I sat there for an hour, just meditating, watching the water and thinking about my life here on the coast.

Five more minutes passed, and then I felt sick to my stomach. I covered my mouth with my hand and barely made it to the bathroom. I was power hurling, and the tears were running down my face. I couldn't get my breath because the heaving wouldn't stop. I sat there puking for at least twenty minutes before I could move from the toilet. I called up to Alec, and he finally came down a few minutes later. He felt fine, he said and told me to go lie down. It's food poisoning, he said, and it would pass; it would just take time. He brought me up a glass of water and a pail in case I couldn't make it to the bathroom in time. He set the pail next to the bed on the floor and told me that he would sleep in the other room so as not to disturb me, and then he kissed me on the forehead and left.

I was sick a few more times that night and vowed to never, ever touch Chilean sea bass again. Alec went back to work as usual the next day, and I sat around the house. I decided to go down to the beach and swim, work out my tight muscles that were screaming for relief. I sat at the beach for a few minutes and drank my green goddess smoothie. The water was calm and clear, and I watched as two dolphins played back and forth a few feet from shore. The water was that gorgeous blue-green that you can see through. I walked into the water up to my waist and stood there, my arms moving back and forth in the water, longing to swim and keep swimming until I could reach the edge of the horizon. I inhaled deeply and closed my eyes…and felt sick to my stomach.

My smoothie kept rising up in my throat, and I didn't want to throw up in that beautiful water. I ran back and grabbed the plastic bag that had held my drink and barfed into that. I'm never sick, and I thought that the Chilean sea bass incident had been over.

I packed my things into my duffel bag and headed home. I felt clammy, and the nausea was coming infrequently in waves. The smell of the ocean seemed to have changed, and it made me gag. It took me about ten minutes of calculations before it finally set in. I didn't have food poisoning. I was pregnant.

I swung by the pharmacy on the corner of 41 and crept in to buy a pregnancy kit. I had seen them at the dollar tree for a buck, but nope, it may tell me I'm having an alien. I'd rather pay full price and get real results. So, the test is tucked nicely into the plastic bag, and I head up to the spare bathroom to take it, nervous, yet almost giddy with anticipation. This is what we've been waiting for, I thought to myself, but I think my biggest hope would be that, if I was finally preggers, Alec would maybe, just maybe, spend a little more time at home and a little less time traveling.

I sat the test aside after doing my business on it, and I waited. It didn't take long, and the two bright pink dots surfaced from the white, and I didn't know what to do. Laugh, scream, cry? So many thoughts were running through my head. Alec was at work, and I didn't want to give him the news over the phone, and there was really no one else I could tell. It's like having this big juicy secret and standing on the mountain ready to shout it out in supreme joy, only to look down into the silence and see only puffy clouds moving by aimlessly. It was pathetic to imagine, and that made me sad. I put the test back into its box and put it in my underwear drawer, my mind spinning with the possibilities of how I'd spring it on Alec.

I finally decided to make him my homemade lasagna that he had once said he loved so much. I didn't like turning on the oven in this heat, but heck, it was a special occasion, and that called for sacrifice. I made a grocery list and went down to Publix to pick up the supplies, found a beautiful bouquet that had tons of baby's breath in it, and went to the bakery to get a loaf of bread to go with dinner. I grabbed two pastries while I was there, figuring that to hell with the diet, I'm splurging and eating for two now. I'm going to grow a basketball looking belly with a child tucked away neatly inside in the coming months, so the dieting would have to wait.

I got home and threw it all together effortlessly. My state was pure joy, and I felt so alive. We made a life, and I was ready to do backflips on the floor, not that I'd be capable of that, ever. I washed all my dishes and set the table with the good china, put the flowers in the middle of the table in a vase, and went to take a shower.

I stood in the bathroom, naked in front of the mirror, and looked at my body. I had come so far. I didn't look like the fat girl anymore; my curves were softer and moving in the right directions. I touched my stomach, stroking it gently, and said hello to the baby that was tucked away like a little pea in the pod. I was going to be a mom, finally, and I cried, aware of the future that would be growing within me for the next 8 months.

Alec came home tired and in one of his moods. You know the one that men often have, where nothing brings joy, and everything you do is looked at like nothing. I often wondered if it was just my insecurities slipping out into the open, but today, I wasn't in the mood to deal with him or his negative shit. I had more than me to be concerned with now, and I'd always believed your mood can affect others in good ways or bad. We wake with the choice each day, and I knew now that tomorrow would be a new beginning for me and our baby.

I sat at the table and waited for Alec to join me. He looked at the bread basket and raised his eyebrows. I hadn't had bread at the table in over two years.

"What's the occasion? Decide to jump off the wagon completely? Does this mean we can have fun eating again?" I wasn't rising to the bait, and I just smiled at him and held my breath.

"I thought it would be nice. Would you like a glass of wine?" He shook his head no and pulled up a seat, then changed his mind and grabbed the bottle, filling his glass three quarters of the way full.

"Aren't you having any?" he asked and looked at the glass of lemonade in front of me. I shook my head no and scooped up some lasagna.

"Okay, what's going on? Bread, lasagna, you do know how many calories are in this shit, right? You were doing so good, so something must be wrong that you're throwing away all that hard work for this." His hands motioned towards the spread on the table. I grabbed his plate and scooped him up some and sat it in front of him. He took a big gulp of the wine and then another.

"I had a really shitty day at work, and I've got to go back in this evening. I'll probably stay at Brett's. An emergency case came in, and time is of the essence. I'm sorry, but I'll have to eat and run."

I looked at him, knowing this was typical for him lately, and for a second, I wondered if there was somebody else. We hadn't made love since the night on the boat, and every day he seemed more distant, but dammit, we'd worked for this moment to happen, and there was no time like the present to tell him.

"We're going to have a baby. I'm pregnant" I said with my brightest smile, and he almost choked on the lasagna he was chewing on. His eyes grew wide, and he looked downright scared for a minute, and then he got a huge grin on his face, jumped up and hugged me tight.

"Oh my God, we're going to have a baby. How amazing is that?" He had tears in his eyes, and I felt okay about everything again. We sat back down, and I told him about the beach incident and then I ran and got the pregnancy test and showed it to him. He was crying, and I felt good, like I was finally able to be a real woman, a real wife to him.

We finished up dinner, and he skipped desert, having to get back to Tampa for his surgery. He kissed me goodbye and smiled, and he held me tight while I cried my tears of happiness, then he turned, grabbed his keys off the hook, and left.

I cleaned up after dinner, wrapped up the leftovers, and ate only half of my pastry. I went up to the office, and grabbed the copy I had bought two years earlier of What to Expect When You're Expecting. I couldn't wait to see what I could expect. I patted my belly and sang to the little nymph that was somewhere in my middle sea, floating on my water and dreaming, I hoped, of a life filled with love.

Chapter Eleven

A Mermaids legacy...a beach ball belly does, in fact, float.

Dear Kate,

I would like to say that being pregnant was a whole lot of fun, but morning sickness swept me away, not only in the morning, but in the afternoon and evening too. My hope of seeing more of Alec was soon dashed. Nothing changed, and though he tried to be as supportive as he could, work was always calling him away. He looked to me to take care of the details. It was a lonely existence, but I refused to be sad. My baby needed me.

I found a good doctor and explained what had happened years ago with Alia, so they were monitoring me more closely, I think, than one would normally be watched. At least now they knew my history. At two months in, they detected two heart beats. I was having twins. What was an amazing present had now doubled itself.

I waited another month before I told Alec, not wanting to freak him out, and with the miscarriage before, I didn't want to jinx anything, in case something bad happened. I know. Think positive thoughts, but I always seemed to be waiting for the other shoe to drop.

We pulled one of the guest rooms to turn it into a nursery, and I spent hours looking at color swatches, fabrics, and of course, not knowing if it was to be girls or boys, held off on making the final decision until later. The morning sickness finally abated, and everything was going swimmingly, and when I was five months along, I walked into Dr. Abrams office for my sonogram reveal. Alec had only been able to make the last one, so I went in alone, eager to learn which of my decorating dreams would come to fruition. I lay there as the cold jelly was spread over my ever-expanding abdomen, and I watched on the monitor with tears in my eyes. I must say I was startled to find I was getting one of each.

I knew that both color options would now work, and I'd have to decide if they'd each get their own room or keep them together for the first year. The room was huge, and I could easily fit two cribs in, and after being together for nine months, it might keep them more comfortable having each other's voices in the same atmosphere again.

I hefted my ass off the table and thanked the doctor. They were now going to bump up the frequencies of my checkups because the boy was a little smaller than the girl. They checked for genetic markers for Downs Syndrome and other things that I couldn't even wrap my mind around, and it all looked good.

Alec called and wasn't coming home, so I told him the news over the phone, and he seemed excited or as excited as Alec can possibly be. I went out and wallowed around in the pool for a little while, my belly buoyant even though I felt like I was a cow, then I got changed and headed to the paint store.

Ocean colors in sea foam/turquoise were what I had fallen in love with, and the view of their room was of the blue green ocean. My little mer-people were chugging along nicely, and now I had to ponder names. I'd like to say Alec helped, but when I brought it up, he just told me to pick something, and he'd either like it or hate it, but he trusted my judgement. I was a bit pissed about that.

I was seeing that the future would hold mostly me and them, and that I'd be doing most of the work. I told him how I felt, and then he was critical and denied it, then he was angry. Granted, he was the sole bread winner for the house, but come on, it took two to make a life, and I'd appreciate a little help. He said he'd see what he could do, but I realized at that moment that nothing was going to change.

I vowed that, no matter what, I was going to appreciate my children and raise them in happiness with all the love I could muster. I was surprised the next day when a delivery truck pulled up with a large wooden crate. The man asked if I was Destiny, and I was shocked. I hadn't ordered anything that big for the nursery yet, and he said he was given orders to unpack it in the back garden. I showed him where the garden was, and he and another big, muscular guy hauled it to the backyard edge. Their crowbars ripped into the wood, and packed away inside was a beautiful sculpture.

It was a mermaid rising from a flowing wave, and she was reaching up for a dolphin that was suspended over her head. Her face was pure ecstasy, and I burst into tears. I asked who it was from, but they had no information. They picked up all the pieces of the crate, wished me a good day, and drove away. I touched her smooth skin and cried like a baby, wondering who would bestow such a splendid gift on me.

Alec called later and told me that it was from him, his way of apologizing for being such a shit heel. I forgave him, and I sat out there later, pulling up a chair and just gazing at her, wishing for a moment that I was thin and beautiful again. The babies were moving around and being very active. I pictured them being like a yin and yang symbol, side by each, moving in harmony, and I felt peace for the first time in days.

The room was coming along nicely. Baby furniture seemed to be arriving almost daily, and the men would carry it up and move it as I arranged the little child paradise in my mind. I painted some fish on the walls, bright colorful salt water creatures, breaking them in early to the life of being mer-children. My hopes were as high as the sky, and nothing could break my spirit.

At six months, I went in for another sonogram, and it was another indication that something may be wrong. The girl was developing on schedule, but the boy was falling behind where he should have been. His heartbeat wasn't as strong, and I was advised to spend more time resting. I still swam every day, but I was going to do what I could to help him along. Two weeks later, there was very little change. I tried to stay positive, but with each visit, my hopes were growing slimmer and slimmer.

At seven months, I began to grow scared. He was floundering, and there wasn't anything I could do about it, and three weeks later, my worst fears became my new reality.
Alec was of course working, and I began to have contractions. I had made it to almost eight months, but something was wrong. Very, very wrong. I woke up from a troubled sleep and could barely move, and I was bleeding; the pain was unbearable. I tried to get ahold of Alec, leaving message after message to no avail. I called the doctor, and he told me to call an ambulance. He'd meet me there.

I remember crying between screaming, and they told me I needed an emergency C-section. Everything went blank once I heard someone say that they were only detecting one heartbeat.

Leila Sirena Montgomery was born at 2:15 a.m., and Liam Nicholas Montgomery was stillborn.

Chapter Twelve

The best day becomes the worst day of my life.

Alec finally made it in four hours after the event, and they had me pretty well sedated. Leila was in the natal unit. Her heartbeat was strong, and she was a little fighter. The doctor told me she was doing very well at five and a half pounds.

I insisted on holding Liam one last time before they took him away. I touched his tiny little feet and kissed his precious sleeping face, telling him how sorry I was, and how I wasn't ready to say goodbye. I didn't want to let him go when they came for him. They gave me a shot to calm me down. I remember dreaming that we were all swimming together in the gulf. They were both beautiful, happy toddlers, with silver blonde hair, chubby little legs, and wide smiles. Liam kept showing me the fish that swam near his feet.

"Fishies, mommy, look, fishies," and he'd giggle in that sweet little boy voice, and I said, "Yes, love, fishies, sweet swimming fishies." I tousled his hair, and he waved at me once, and then he slipped into the wave and disappeared. I woke screaming for him, and once again, they sedated me.

I woke to Alec beside me, holding my hand. He was sobbing quietly, and I realized that I didn't care. He saw that I was awake, and he stroked my cheek lightly.

"It's gonna be all right, Dest. We'll get you a boy next time. It's gonna be okay, and I saw Leila. She is amazing and beautiful, just like you." I closed my eyes and drifted away again, leaving him far behind as I swam to the horizon.
They released me four days later, and Alec was actually there to take me home with our baby girl. I had told him not to touch the nursery, knowing I had to deal with things in my own way. I walked slowly into the house carrying Leila and found dozens of flowers all over the house from friends and coworkers of Alec. It was nice, but it reminded me of a funeral. We were going to hold a quiet service for Liam when we were ready, having had him cremated. It would happen in the future when I was able to do it without breaking down. I refused to think about where I would have him interred. I just wanted him close by me for a while longer.

With Alec gone for most of the pregnancy, I knew it was my choice in how to grieve. I gave no say to his wishes. Liam was mine, and I was going to say goodbye in my own way.

Leila was a very good baby. She rarely cried, and when she did, it was out of hunger or just wanting to be coddled. She loved being held close to my heart, and I wondered if she missed Liam as much as I did. She had been his yang to his yin, and I hoped she would allow me to be his replacement.

Her eyes were a beautiful shade of blue, and her silver blonde curls grew so fast. I took to being a mother like a fish in the sea, and I relished spoiling my baby girl. I dismantled the extra crib two weeks after I got home and added more girly elements to the room. The baby clothes he would have worn were donated to a women's shelter, and I scattered his ashes in my beloved sea.

I knew I'd hear him every time the waves moved, and it felt right. I didn't want a reminder of what I'd lost, a permanent place in the ground where I'd have to visit him and be sad. I let him go, a small fistful of grey ashes on a beautiful morning as the sun peeked over the horizon, casting its light on the soft delicate waves that would always speak his name to me.

I suppose I was going through postpartum depression. I was unable to breast feed, which tore my heart up, but I decided I was going to be the mother that mine had never been. Leila would never want for love, because I had all the time in the world to dote on her.

Alec became absent again, and that was fine with me. He hadn't been a husband in quite some time, and he was angry with me when I made the decision that I did not want Leila to know that her twin had died while she had survived. Kids have enough to deal with, I reasoned, and I wasn't going to lay that on her. I felt justified in my decision. Why should Leila have to have survivor's guilt for the rest of her life? Alec finally relented and agreed.

Leila was growing daily it seemed, and we would swim around as I held her tight, swishing her little butt around in the blue water. She loved the water as much as I did, and her giggle lit up my world. I thought that she would grow up to be a lot like me in a lot of ways, but better, and I loved her more than life itself, doing everything in my power to never let her feel alone.

2018

Dear Kate,

I found you today while cleaning out the desk, and I can't believe how much time has passed since we last spoke. I'd say I'm sorry, but I've been busy living my best life. Nothing has changed with Alec. He's getting older, but aren't we all?

Leila is in high school and will be graduating in a few months. She's strong-willed and beautiful, she has more friends than I can count, and her grades are off the charts. It seems we did something right after all. I've never seen such a positive kid, really. She's given us our headaches, and when she learned to drive, boy, that was an experience I never want to have to go through again in this lifetime.

Alec is still absent. He was given a promotion at work a few years ago and is now the head of neurosurgery. I attend the functions that I have to, smiling and pretending that we are the happy couple, but I know we just circle around each other's lives and co-exist like the sun and moon.

Something good has come of it all, though. I've learned to live my own life. I've taken some classes in watercolor painting, and guess what my specialty is, yep, mermaids. I think I do pretty well, but I do mostly seascapes, shells, and a lot of beach things.

Leila and I have gone to look at some colleges, and for some reason, I think I'm more excited about it than she is. She excels in business and art. She is heavily involved in equestrian, and she has a horse named Frito that we keep boarded a few miles away. When she rides, it's as if she and that horse become one. I don't know how to describe it, but it's an amazing thing to witness. I thought she'd go for equestrian medicine, but at some point along the way, she changed her mind. Whatever will make her happy, I'm fine with it. Alec has been socking money away since she was born, so wherever she decides to go, she won't be saddled with student loans for the rest of her life.

I say a prayer for Liam every day when I rise and see the waves, and we still have never told Leila. I think we made the right call. I hate secrets. They can destroy so easily and the last thing I'd ever want to do is hurt my sweet Leila. We are close, and it's almost like we're best friends. We have a healthy respect for each other, and I think I did a damn fine job raising her to be her own person.

I've got to run, and I'll tell you more when I can. I guess I just stopped by to fill you in and say hello to my dear old friend once more.

Dear Kate,

In the flick of an eye, everything can be stolen away. Fate plays the cruelest cards when she chooses, and I am standing here holding a crappy hand. I don't know where to begin, and I am lost for the first time in years. I've lived my life, excelled at gaining my confidence, and raised a beautiful girl singlehandedly through all of life's ups and downs.

My world is falling apart, and I need help. I know that I have had a good life. It wasn't perfect, but it wasn't bad. I had my baby girl and a beautiful house and unlimited funds to do anything I wanted to do for the last twenty plus years. I don't know what the future will hold, and I'm suddenly scared.

Alec is dead. He and Brett were driving back from Orlando on Interstate 95, and a semi stopped in front of them. Either they weren't paying attention or, I don't know, but they plowed into the back of it doing 90 miles per hour, according to the police. The Porsche flew right beneath the semi, and the whole thing went up in flames. The truck driver also died. Alec and Brett both died instantly. I know he hasn't been here for most of our marriage, but I did love him. I was proud of the work he did at the hospital, and everyone is just devastated.

Leila is on a trip to Scotland, and she's been calling occasionally to tell me all about her excursions. I don't want to ruin it for her. The news will have to wait until she gets home. I'm letting her enjoy her last hurrah before college and don't want to rush her back here. There's nothing she can do to change it.

Alec was never sure if he wanted to be cremated, which is pretty much what he ended up doing regardless, and Leila will be back next week, and I'll break it to her then.

Is that selfish of me, do you think? I tried to put myself in her shoes, and I think I would want to be home to hear the news, not rushing home because of it. I don't know, but the decision has been made and that's that. I'll cross the bridge with her when she returns.

I had to go into his office at the hospital and clear out his desk of personal effects a few days after he passed, and when you thought life couldn't get any worse, it goes right on ahead and tosses you around some more.

I found the box of letters in his closet. It didn't take much reading to realize that he and Brett had been lovers and had been for most of our marriage, if not before. I have to break it to Leila, along with the news of his being gone permanently. I really am at a loss as to what to say. It does explain a lot, but for all the years I thought something was wrong with me, I find out that he just loved someone else more.

I found stacks of the love letters, and after I read a few, I stormed out of his office and confronted his secretary about his life-long affair. I asked her, as I sobbed with my heart breaking, and as I held up the letters in a tight fist, if what I was seeing was true, and the look on her face spoke volumes. My husband was gay, and I never knew it. I didn't know what to think.

Why did he stay with me for all these years? How could he do this to me? To our daughter? I'm mad and so angry for this, this lie. I like to think I would have rather let him go live out his true life, but then I realized that, had I done that, I wouldn't have Leila now.

You live with someone for years, you think you know pretty much everything you possibly could, and then you find that your entire marriage was a lie. How do you move on from that?

His insurance policy will cover us for the rest of our lives, but I feel like my life has been a big charade. I've been a housewife forever, and I've set everything on the back burner for my husband and daughter, only to find out it was a lie. Damn him and damn Brett!

Hey Kate,

I need to breathe. I've really got to focus and think about what to do. Leila just got back from her trip, and I still think I made the right call by not wanting to ruin it by bringing her home. It didn't change anything except buying me some time to figure out what the hell to tell her. She's out riding Frito. She'll be home shortly, and I've got to tell her about Alec before she hears about it some other way. When she got home from her trip, she didn't even ask how he was. That's the way it's been for too long now.

How do you break your daughter's heart?

How do you heal your own?

Chapter Thirteen

Swimming forward, in to the great blue open.

I've got time to kill before she comes home, and I really have to calm down. Maybe I'll tell you a little about Leila, frame her for you. I went so long without talking to you that I see I didn't say much about her.

I remember when Leila got her first pony. Her name was Daisy, and she was the gentlest creature in the world. Leila had to have been around seven. I wonder why I don't remember. It was a huge day, and Alec was surprisingly home that weekend for her birthday. We dressed her in jeans, which for Florida in the summer is not fun at all, and I remember she was very angry.

She wanted to wear her party dress, and she kicked up a fuss about having to wear those pants. Alec told her, if she didn't behave, then he was going to throw out her cake and ice cream and that she'd have to have a tuna fish sandwich. If Leila hated anything, it was tuna fish sandwiches, one way in which she is not like me. So, she capitulated but still stomped up to her room like a little drama queen. Boom Boom Boom went her little bare feet as they went slapping up the stairs, and her cheeks were a bright red as she huffed and puffed. I remember she made it about halfway up then turned around, hands on her hips and stated matter of fact, "It had better be a damn good present or I'm never speaking to either of you ever again."

Oh boy! Alec glanced at me, assuming that I had taught her that word, and I was trying so hard not to laugh. He looked at her and gave her five-seconds to go change her clothes or the birthday would be cancelled. He must have looked like he meant business, because she turned and high-tailed it up the stairs two at a time, reappearing a few minutes later. She was all geared up in her little designer jeans, her sparkly purple vest, and cowgirl boots and hat. We had told her only that she was going for a ride on a horse for her birthday, not that she was getting one of her own.

We drove down to the stables where Daisy was waiting. She watched the roads we were traveling on and had no idea why we were going this way. This wasn't the place she normally would go to ride a horse, and she looked confused when we pulled in.

Leila flung the car door open with gusto, and Alec stopped her before she could go too far. He asked her where she had learned the word damn. Well, she looks at him as sweet as pie and says, "I learned it from you, Daddy. You were on the phone and said it two times. I counted, one, two."

She held up two fingers as if to add an extra flourish to her statement, and I was cracking up. So, there you go, Alec. Mom isn't the bad guy after all, ha! He told her it was a bad word and not to say it anymore. She looked at me and winked. She was a crafty kid, that one, and she and I were always best pals. I'm sure Alec wondered for a while after that when he could have said it, and I just let him ponder, knowing full well that she learned it from me. I'm crafty like that, too.

When she saw Daisy, she cried. Excitement flooded through her, and she hugged that sweet pony so tightly I was worried she'd hurt it. It had a big Happy Birthday, I'm Yours banner around its neck. Leila and that little horse were inseparable for the next six years, and when she outgrew her, she was given to a family with two little girls who would continue to spread the love to that beautiful pony.

I hear the garage door opening. She's home. I'm crying already. Wish me luck.

Dear Kate,

That was one of the most difficult things I've ever done. Leila took it better than I did about Alec and Brett being a couple, but the fact that they were both now gone tore her up.

She understood why I didn't bring her home from the trip, and I know it will take her time to heal.

Alec and I had two burial plots together that he had purchased years ago. This, of course, was after I told him that I wanted to be cremated and scattered in the ocean. He always listened well, ha! They were beneath a beautiful oak tree down in the local cemetery, and I asked Leila if she was okay with me giving up my spot so that Alec and Brett could be together. She agreed. I had no desire to be next to him, instead, going back to my original plan of being scattered in the ocean with Liam.

Leila went upstairs, and I went out to sit on the patio and watch my waves, communing mentally with Liam. A sailboat was out on the horizon, and with the distance, it seemed to be moving so slowly.

I felt like that boat most days, distant and just moving in slow motion towards something that I couldn't see. I closed my eyes and inhaled the tang of the salty air and felt a calm flow through me. Telling her the news was hard. I've never been one to enjoy turmoil and realizing how little time Alec spent in our lives when he was here, each day since his passing had still felt almost normal, except for hearing the sound of his voice. I missed that.

I suppose I could have just told myself he's at work, but I knew the void in my heart was more from the betrayal. I searched my memory for any clues I could have missed, and I came up with absolutely nothing. I couldn't beat myself up for what he had done, but I felt so empty. I looked over at the mermaid sculpture in the garden and knew that he had always seen me as that mermaid, joyful and strong. I knew I needed to find her again.

Leila came down a short time later and joined me. She held a glass of Pinot Grigio, her long fingernails were freshly painted. She had graduated a month earlier, and I asked her if she still wanted to have her party. I couldn't see her eyes behind the mirrored lenses of her sunglasses, but I could tell she had been crying. We had always let her drink at home once she turned sixteen, but only if she wasn't going anywhere. We had been young once upon a time, and knowing that she was going to do it anyway, we'd rather she drank where we could monitor her. She was never the party girl type, and we respected her judgement. She took a sip and sat it down on the table beside her. Maybe it was the memory of the lunch box thermoses. I just didn't want her to have to hide things away as she was finding herself. Teen years sucked the big one, from everything that I could remember. Why make it more difficult?

"I don't want to have the party, Mom. They're mostly Dad's friends, and only a few of mine are able to come. They just want to give me money for college, and I don't feel comfortable taking their gifts for something I don't think I'll use." It took me a minute to realize there was something in that explanation that I was missing.

"I don't get it, Leila. Why don't you think you'll use their gifts? I know we're good for the money for school, but this could be your spending money. They're excited for you, and not everyone gets accepted to such a prestigious school. You'll love Harvard." She took her sunglasses off and looked me in the eye.

"I've been thinking a lot about it, Mom, while I was in Scotland and when I was out riding Frito earlier. I'm not going to go to school, not yet, anyway. There's so much out there in the world that I want to see, places I want to explore, and if I go to

110

school, I'm afraid I'll never get the chance to live my life the way I want to. I know that you're thinking I'm crazy, and with Dad...gone, I hate the idea of leaving you alone, but it's just something I need to do while I can. When I'm older, I won't be able to enjoy it as much. Are you mad?" She took another sip of wine and waited for my response.

I looked out at the water and didn't know what to think. I thought back to when I was her age and wondered, if I had the chance to do it all over again, would I have done it any differently? Life was hard for me, and she had it easy. She's never wanted for anything, and who was I to tell her what to do? Yes, I'd love her to go to school, but I also know how fragile this life that we live can be. How could I say no to my baby wanting to live her best life in her own way? It was her choice, not mine, and I couldn't bring myself to tell her no.

I smiled at her, my eyes tearing up, and I told her she had my blessing. I could see it as the stress physically left her body. She leaned over and hugged me tight, and I felt my tears fall freely on her beautiful blouse. I apologized for the wet spot, and we laughed. She wiped at her tears. I asked her where she was planning to go, and she got excited then ran in and grabbed a big notebook.

She came back out and plopped down in her chair and opened it up to the center of the book. There were pages filled with notes and scribbles in the margins, just like she had done when she was a child. There were at least ten pages filled with the names of the places she wanted to go, what she wanted to eat in each country, and I realized she must have been planning this for quite a while. If I was younger, I might have been jealous, but I was thrilled for her. I was imagining her hiking across

Europe, walking along the many miles of Camino de Santiago, and she was strong enough to do it all.

I knew she was smart and would be careful, and then she told me that her girlfriend Julia was going along with her. I liked Julia, and she'd been one of those children who had been around the world with her parents, so who better to travel with than someone who knew the basics?

I was getting hungry, and we went out for a bite to eat. The prepped dinner in the fridge could wait, and I felt like celebrating. I was happy for her. I would spend tomorrow calling everyone to cancel the party, and she offered to do it for me. I let her take on that chore, and she looked confident. At some point in the last year, she had grown up. I was proud of the woman I had raised and felt that I couldn't have done a better job.

Hey Aunt Kate,

It's been a whirlwind getting Leila ready for her trip, and I'm just now finding time to sit and talk to you. I know you understand; you always understand. We went out and did a lot of shopping for items that she needed to take with her and had a lot of mother/daughter bonding moments. I'm not sure when she'll be back.

I treated myself to a new hairstyle yesterday. I had it permed and frosted, and now I'm mostly blonde. Some days I feel like it too. The other day, I accidentally bought two of the same necklaces for Leila, and I ended up keeping the extra one for myself. It has a Celtic tree of life pendant in sterling silver on a fine silver chain. I told her it was me, rooted deep, yet always there to provide shelter. I knew I had seen it and admired it somewhere. I guess that my mind is not firing on all cylinders, but I have a pretty new necklace because of it.

She leaves in two days, and I feel sad, knowing I'm going to miss her something fierce. She told me, if she stays somewhere long enough, I can fly over and join her, but I don't see her planting herself anywhere for very long. It's not her style. She's on a mission to grasp her future, and it's always moving in a forward direction. We can talk on the phone and just play it by ear after that.

I cleaned out all of Alec's belongings from the house, donated his clothes to a men's shelter and his books to the hospital for the Neurology department. I buried his letters with him, and Brett is lying beside him, dead together and now resting in peace together. I think he would have appreciated that. I'm trying to be the bigger person about it, but I'm still so very angry. You can't choose who you love, but it harkens back to the days of my youth, the lying and such.

Before you ask, no, I never told Leila about Liam. I guess I'm the pot calling the kettle black.

The party was cancelled, but people sent Leila checks for her graduation. So many cards came wishing her well in her future, and she felt loved by everyone. She tucked the money into her bank account, alongside the cash I transferred from our "college fund" account. She will use it wisely, and maybe she will go to school, either here or overseas. Whatever she wants to do, I know she'll succeed; that's just her way.

Hey Kate,

I don't think I've cried as much in the last year as I have this past month. I dropped Leila off at the airport last night. She's excited, her energy is high, and I'm happy for her yet sad for me. I realized it after I drove away. In two weeks, it will be her eighteenth birthday, and it's the first time we won't be together for her special day. She said she'll call and we can toast over the phone, but it's just not the same. I am sitting here watching the waves as I write this and realize that it means Liam will have been gone for that long, too. Where does the time go? It seems like yesterday they were just on the verge of arrival, then one came and the other...well, you know, and now Leila departs for the unknown world that waits for her, and I'm here wondering what comes next.

I will be 54 next week too. Our birthdays are only a week apart, and that's another day that won't be shared together. I don't really celebrate my birthday anymore. Getting older sucks, and tacking on another year to it isn't that much of a thrill to me at this point. One more year until double nickels, and I don't see anything changing for me anytime soon.

My psychiatrist has recommended a pill to take the edge off these flip-flopping episodes of sadness. I told her I'm not suicidal and that I refuse to be medicated. I've been strict on my goals as far as keeping the weight off, although I did gain a few after Alec died. But having Leila around has kept me, out of necessity, making healthy choices for meals, and now with her gone, I don't want to relapse.

I did buy some donuts, with the weak excuse that it's an easy breakfast. I mean, why cook one egg for one person? But when I opened the box, the smell of the grease turned me off. I went right back out, drove into town, and handed the box off to the group of homeless people that congregate in the park. I figured it was better than throwing them into the garbage, and they seemed to appreciate it.

I don't know, Kate. I just feel lost these days. Like that sailboat that appears on the horizon but is missing the sail. If you come up with any ideas, please let me know. I have nothing but will sit down again and try to come up with a list of what I would like to learn/accomplish in the next year. I do very well when I have them written down. I don't have to try to remember that way.

Chapter Fourteen

The list of tomorrow...a mermaid makes a plan.

Happy Birthday to me, although I don't know what is so happy about it. I've been working on my list, and gratitude is first up. Wake every day with a grateful heart. So, I am grateful to be here in this beautiful house. I am grateful that I have my health. I am grateful that I look okay for my age. Is that enough? I hope so. I'm just grateful; let's leave it at that.

So, I went in for my yearly checkup yesterday and got the shock of my life. I had to sit in the waiting area and fill out that asinine form they give to you. I laugh every time, because nothing ever changes from one year to the next. If it did, don't you think they'd figure out that your doctor would be the one initiating the changes? Any new drugs? Any surgeries? It's a grand waste of time is what I think it is. But…when I got to the section of last menstrual period, I kind of went blank. I couldn't remember.

I pulled out my mini-calendar that I keep in my purse and went back month by month. It's the only way I could ever keep track. I refused to put it in my cell phone, because if I ever lost it, how embarrassing would that be? Gee, what are these five little stars for every month? I don't know, could it be her monthly? So, I go back, and then back a little farther, and I realize it has been over eight months since that crafty bitch Mother Nature has been by for a visit.

Now I know obviously that I'm not pregnant. If I was, it would be an immaculate conception. If one hasn't had sex in too many years to count, that kind of leaves pregnancy out of the equation. Then I started freaking out a bit. What if it's cancer? I had myself so worked up by the time I got in to see her that I was convinced I was dying tomorrow.

My doctor is always pretty serious, and she asked me a few questions in general about changes. Was I having hot flashes? Was I having mood swings? I shook my head, trying to remember. Mood swings were an easy one. Having lost my husband, who was a closet gay man, mind you, and then having your daughter skip college to run away to tour the world, well, my moods have been off the charts. Why do you ask? I tried to be pleasant about it, but all I could think about was Cancer with a capital C.

Then I remembered a few times of being overcome by walls of heat. I had been blaming it on the Florida temperatures and the humidity that constantly fluctuated. I always slept in a cool to the point of icy bedroom at night because, otherwise, I would wake up in a puddle. I didn't realize it could be hot flashes.

She welcomed me to the wonderful world of menopause, almost confirming it when she went to do my pelvic and I was dry to the point of pain. Normally that sucker would slide right in with the cold goo she used, but this time, no go. I'm in the throes of menopause. I think I'll take that over the cancer thing, but I felt like a dried up old lady when those words finally sunk in.

I guess that explains the chin hairs growing out of control that, if left alone, would give me the face of a sea otter, and we won't talk about the one white pubic hair I "not so gracefully" yanked out with my needle nose tweezers a few weeks ago. That was painful, perhaps a wheat thresher next time. I wanted to cry. I wanted to crawl in a hole and just be done with it all but not really. I'm not suicidal, just tired.

Do they sell a book on that? Kind of like the baby one, but what to expect when you hit menopause? I will have to google it later, although I think I'd be embarrassed to order it. Our mailman is kind of hot, and I had an issue once when I ordered off Amazon. The paper bag they sent it in ripped a little, exposing the cover. It was a murder mystery and nothing sleazy, thank God. It was a good thing it wasn't fifty shades of porn or anything like that; that would be downright tragic and embarrassing. I would have had to move. The mailman apologized but said, if it was damaged, report it to Amazon, that they were pretty good about that. I guess they use USPS too these days.

I left the doctor's office a short time later and headed for the Goodwill bookstore on 41. I perused the sections until I found the self-help girly book area and found a ton of books on the subject. The checkout person was a girl, so I felt comfortable going through and buying the most promising looking ones then added another spiritual healing one. I needed all the help I could get.

Here I am, 54 years old and now barren. I had never thought of more children, and I know that some women can still have them at my age. It's just the fact that that ship has sailed; there will be no more eggs, no more babies. It made me tear up a little, and I realized that I didn't know where to go or what to do from here. I realized that I could've cared less about sex. After Alec went to work and was never around, the thought kind of faded after a while. I was busy. I had a home to handle and a baby to raise.

I suppose I'll cross that bridge later, but in the meantime, the dating thing just doesn't appeal in the least. What I would like is a girlfriend to be able to do things with, though, to gossip over lunch and shop with, but a man? I can't even imagine it. Maybe it's because I can't trust my judgement. Maybe it's that I can't trust, period. I don't know. Maybe there's a book that can magically transform my attitude. I'll check next time I'm in the self-help section.

Making friends is first on my list. I found a free group that gets together on Saturdays down in the park. I'm not worried about money, but free is good, and maybe I'll find good quality people there who will be down to earth. After years of being in the midst of doctors, their snobby uptight wives, and the upper echelon of society, I need a break from the falseness I found there.

The class I found is called Laughter Yoga. I was walking by Centennial Park the other day, and I watched them. I sat far back on a bench and just smiled as I saw their fun antics. They seemed like they were having a good time. I didn't feel up to joining in, but after their session broke up, I ambled over and asked what it was all about. These ladies had such an enormous amount of happy energy, you could feel it from where I had been sitting. It was like the flu, contagious, but in a good way. I told them I may come down some Saturday and join in. I just needed to think about it. They introduced themselves and seemed very welcoming. I may just do it. If nothing else, I need a laugh to lighten my mood.

There's also a different group that does yoga on the beach. I've always been intrigued by yoga. It seems like a spiritual experience, and these people are so flexible. These days, I'm lucky if I can bend over and tie my shoes without breathing heavy. It is real yoga, unlike the laughter kind, with the stretching, poses, and all that. I stopped by and watched that class for a few minutes, and most of them seemed like they knew what they were doing. I know nothing about yoga. So, the next stop was to the pawn shop to look at DVD's and see if I could pick up one on yoga. I'm not joining until I have some idea as to what the hell I'm doing. I don't need to tip over and do a face plant in the sand and be ridiculed. I like to look competent.

The next on the list of experiences to try was the drum circle down on Nokomis beach. That event I actually enjoyed a lot. I drove down and could hear the beat of the drums before I even got out of my car. There was well over a hundred people there, some dancing and hula-hooping, some drumming, and a lot of people just sitting around watching all the antics. The sun was working its way down to the horizon, and it was beautiful. To hear the drums and watch the day end was perfect in my mind. It felt healing in a way, like a universal heartbeat booming in unison. I don't want to play a drum, but I would someday like to have the courage to get up and dance, freely and uninhibited. I won't be in the belly dancing get-up, but I can wear cottony flowing clothes and look like a hippie from back in the day, like many of the folks I found there.

I realized that I'm like a ghost. Unseen as I wander through the crowds, searching for some connection, for someone to see me. Invisibility is a sad and solitary state, and I've lingered in the limbo for far too long. Some days, I don't recognize myself, and that is sad.

I did finally meet up with one woman when I was there. She was sitting on the outskirts. A bottle of wine was set up on a small make-shift table in front of her, and she saw me watching her. She asked me if I wanted a glass, and I thought, why not?

Her name is Hope, and she's a few years older than me. She has beautiful salt and pepper curly grey hair. She has a genuine smile that can light up a room, and she is just one of the most pleasant souls that I've ever met. She almost reminded me of Pearl, in a way. That's why I was staring at her. There was just something about her that called to me. It was like an ethereal cloud was surrounding her, and it made her stand out. She seems very grounded, and she listens well, or at least she seemed interested in what I had to say.

Her husband passed away in an automobile accident five years ago. She's been through the menopause thing by way of a hysterectomy years ago, and she's had several cancer scares and never had any children. She said she prefers to eat a raw food diet, but she does drink wine occasionally, usually at the drum circle, because she always finds someone to help her drink it. I was jealous. Her face is clear and smooth, with very few wrinkles, and I don't know, she's just sweet. You'd like her. We must have exchanged stories of our lives for two hours, drinking the light, fruity Pinot Grigio and delighting in each other's anecdotes.

At the end of the evening, we exchanged numbers. She seems to keep herself pretty busy, but she promised she'd call this week and we'd go out for lunch. I was excited, and it took me a while to realize it, but it's the first friend I've had since we moved down here. In all these years, I've only had Alec's friends and business associates, no one of my own. It made me happy to know that I did it, something new and just for me. I made a friend.

A week after the drum circle, Hope called me. I don't normally answer the phone unless I recognize the number, but I wasn't thinking and just grabbed it. She had called earlier in the week, but apparently my answering machine never kicked in. Bummer, because I have the cutest message that I worked so hard to get perfect. I'll have to take a look to see what's wrong with it. I hope I haven't missed anything else important.

We are meeting for lunch today, and she suggested going to The Crow's Nest, and I said that sounded good. It's been ages since I've been there, but the food was always quite good, although now with new owners, you just never know. What else have I been doing? Hmmm…let's see. Still trying to keep my weight in check. I think it's going to be a constant battle now, but I won't do the pill route again. Healthy eating and smaller amounts should suffice, I think.

I finally tried the yoga DVD from the pawn shop last night. Some of the moves were easy, but some, good God, it's going to take some time to master it. I'm not going to quit, though. I really need to tune my body back up. I think I need a better wardrobe for doing it, though.

I had on my cotton big girl shorts, and when I went to do the crescent moon pose, they call it the Chandrasana move, according to the silly book that came with the disc, as I went forward to move into the pose, my drawers decided to droop a little too much. If I had been doing this on the beach, my crescent moon would have turned into a full moon. Don't even get me started on the half-bridge. I looked like I was doing the pelvic thrust upwards. For some reason, Jimi Hendrix started singing to me in my head, which isn't exactly a relaxing thought for yoga, and I began singing along, except my words were "excuse me while I hump the sky." I did feel good when I was done, and laughter is most certainly healing.

My doc told me, with the menopause going on, it will be harder to lose weight, so I need to buckle down and start exercising. I am doing laps in the pool every evening, and I had forgotten how good it felt to be immersed in the water. I'm also walking the beach every morning. The sandpipers were clipping along in high speed mode across the sand this morning, and if I were paranoid, I'd almost believe that they were following me. They make me smile, and Alec always had a fondness for them. There have been a lot of pretty shells down there lately, and I'm thinking maybe I should start painting again. I'm trying to fill my days with good things, and it is improving my mood. I've got to go now. Time to get dressed and meet Hope. It's going to be a good day.

Dear Kate,

What a blessing she is, Hope, I mean. She was sitting on the bench waiting for me, and she gave me a big heart to heart hug. We were able to get a window seat, and the view, as always, was spectacular. There were a lot of boats in and out of the jetty, and three dolphins were playing in the wake of the boats that moved through. The water was bright blue, and the sun was blinding. We started with a mimosa, and I listened as Hope told me more about herself.

She's been through a lot, but she's so positive. I realized that circumstances change, shit happens, and it's how we deal with it that defines who we will be. We can let it ruin us, or we can rise up and get over it. I'm choosing to rise. We sat and talked for almost three hours. She likes to kayak through the mangroves, and I've never tried that. She has two kayaks, and we're going to go out this weekend. I'm excited about it, although I worry about alligators. She laughed when I told her that, and she said they're more afraid of us than we are of them. We will see, but I'll let her lead until I get the hang of it. She lives close to me on the island, too, a mere five minutes away.

I went out on a limb and told her how, when I was younger, I wanted to be a mermaid. She didn't laugh, and I was thankful for that. She wanted to be a ballerina and was for many years but decided not to go the pro route once she had married and gotten pregnant. She has had three miscarriages, and I told her about mine and then the death of Liam. She cried as I told her, and she came around the table and hugged me. It felt like I'd lost a hundred-pound weight off my shoulders. I could talk about it and not be falling apart. It is the gains and losses through my history that's made me who I am. I can't forget it, but I can't go back either. She's a godsend, and I am, again, grateful.

I'm having her over for lunch next week and looking forward to it. I will have to get creative in the cooking department, but with the Farmers market on Saturday, I will be able to pick up a lot of fresh fixings.

Leila called me last night, and she's in Peru. From the sounds of it, she's having a ball. She said she'd send me some pictures when she has time, but she's not regretting her decision. I'm happy for her and glad that she's pursuing her dreams. She misses me but said she'd include some selfies she's taken so that I don't forget what she looks like. As if that would ever happen. There's not much else new here, sorry.

Dear Kate,

Hope and I went kayaking this morning. What a trip! I wonder why I'd never looked into doing that before. I know why. It's no fun alone, and Alec wasn't one for any form of boating unless it was a pleasure cruise on a yacht. I only saw one alligator but did find something that gave me the willies.

Mangroves are these trees that come out of the water. They drop more roots down from above and expand almost into tiny islands that way. Someone took the time to clear paths through them, and you maneuver your kayak through these twisting and turning tunnels made of the tree roots.

There's so much greenery back there. It's like being in a foreign jungle. I was doing really well and then I got to an area where I had to put the paddle in my lap and pull myself through by the tree branches, hand over fist. The tide was low, and the kayak made these weird scraping noises as we wriggled our way through. It was so quiet out there. The silence was deafening.

There were these creepy little crabs running up and down the trees. They were so tiny, smaller than a quarter, and I thought they were fake at first until they moved. I almost put my hand on one, and it skittered away. I screamed, and Hope turned to see what was wrong and then she laughed.

I could see starfish down below in the water, and the only thing I found that I didn't like about the experience was realizing that snakes could be up above, twined on the tree branches, and I almost grabbed one when I was pulling my way through. I hate snakes. I sat and nudged it with my paddle to send it on its way and refused to move forward until it made a hasty retreat. I didn't want that sucker falling down on top of me or slithering around in my kayak, or else I'd be in the water after capsizing the craft. Hope waited for me as I waited for Mr. Slithers. She doesn't dislike snakes, but she's not a huge fan either. I'm glad she didn't tell me about them, or I would have never gone with her.

She brought a picnic lunch of cut and sliced fresh veggies and some different varieties of cheeses and crackers. I found out she doesn't live exclusively on raw food. I guess I learned that making assumptions on first meetings isn't a good thing. She found an area in the mangroves where someone had put a picnic table, so we tied up the kayaks and sat there to eat. It was pretty warm out, and you do work up a sweat paddling at times, but I find that, if you splash some of the water on yourself, it helps. It makes your hands really sticky because the water we were in is brackish, but beggars can't be choosers. I'll bring some wet wipes next time because, how was I supposed to know? We drank some water and ate the snacks and then talked more about our lives. We have a lot in common, and I'm glad I met her.

I've been sleeping better at night and still exercising every day. I'm getting more muscular, the jiggles beneath my arms are shrinking, and I don't look like I have chunky chicken skin under there anymore, well, almost none. I'm not noticing much change other than that. I'm just being more cognizant of what I'm eating. Hope recommended meditation to me, and she sent me some links from Hay House. They are like peaceful podcasts without the yammering chitchat. Where do they come up with these things? They seem to do a great job of relaxing me, and they calm my mind. I'm feeling good, and I don't remember being this happy, not in a long time.

Hey Kate,

I am head over heels excited. I was at the beach yesterday, and as is my norm, I was in a chair with my umbrella. I had been swimming for quite a while and then read a trashy romance novel between watching more dolphins frolicking out in the blue. When I was in the water, I went out pretty far this time, but it was calm today, with not much of a breeze or any rip tides, and after a while, I got out and fell asleep with the chair reclined.

I don't know how long I was out, but in my sleep, I felt something tugging on my hair. I jumped when I opened my eyes and looked up. I saw this guy standing over me. His one hand was by my head, and the other held a fishing pole. He jumped back when I screamed, and I yelled at him. I figured he was a perv copping a feel or a homeless man looking for something while I was zonked out. He looked worried and then he apologized.

His fishing hook was caught up in my hair. He was trying to get it out without waking me, and he asked me to hold still as his fingers moved through the curls on the side of my head. He plucked out the hook, taking a few pieces of hair with it, and I saw something blood red and chunky on it. I asked him what the hell it was, and he said squid.

Now I have to go in and rinse squid stink out of my hair, and he followed me, apologizing again for what he had done. I told him it was no big deal, but I dove in the water to clean out any residual crap that may have been left in there. I knew he was standing on shore waiting for me to come out, and once I was satisfied that there was nothing nasty left in my curls, I plodded through the sand and stopped to talk to him.

He was young, but I'm not good at guessing ages, maybe early thirties? He held out his hand and introduced himself. His name was Raphael Santos. He was from Puerto Rico but had moved to the states to live with his sister after Hurricane Maria hit in 2017. He works at one of the resorts up in Siesta Key, but today was his day off. He was around 6'1, which to a girl that's only 5'5 and shrinking, that seems tall. His eyes were a deep chocolate brown and reminded me of those heartbreaking homeless dogs on tv, where they implore you with sadness to get you to send money to the SPCA to save them all. I do send $25 a month to them, by the way. I was always a sucker for puppy dog eyes. He was as cute as a button but way too young for me.

I was intrigued with hearing about Puerto Rico, so I stood there and listened to him as he fished. His voice was soft and had a nice lilt to it. His English was impeccable, and he just exuded this happy charm.

I don't know how to fish and had never possessed a desire to learn, but he showed me how to bait the hook and cast it out. I only snagged a clump of grass on the dunes once, so I could see how he could have gotten my hair easily enough. He had to help me when the line pulled taut, and we ended up catching a big ugly snook. I've eaten snook before, but I wasn't about to take the thing home and learn how to clean and filet it on the fly. It was a keepable size under normal conditions, he said, but was catch and release only because of the red tide last year. I listened to him talk about his homeland while I sat beside him and watched the horizon.

The water was almost up to my toes, and it was getting darker out. The tide was coming in so there wasn't much beach left. The last few storms had eroded a lot of the dunes, and I prefer to come here on low tide when there's more space to lay out without getting your things washed into the ocean.
I lost a good pair of Birkenstocks once that way. They're no good without both of the shoes, and one just wasn't going to cut it. Lessons learned in life. Stay high, stay dry.

I was getting ready to pack it in for the day when he asked me for my number. He wanted to take me fishing in his boat. He promised we wouldn't go far from shore and that we'd be always in sight of land. I shocked myself when I reached into my bag and grabbed my notebook and a pen and gave him my cell number. I mean think about it; here's this really cute guy that you just met who enjoys talking to you, and he wants you to go fishing. Sure, just give out the number and hope he's not a serial killer or something.

I don't have any designs on him or anything, and I really enjoyed his company. It's nice to have someone around to talk to, and I hope I'm not getting too needy and desperate. He did give me his number, too and come to think of it, he never did ask me how old I was. Perhaps I'm a cougar after all...it's that or he's looking for a sugar mama. I don't know, but I guess I will find out.

Chapter Fifteen

Staying high and dry, a mermaid tests the waters.

My pal Kate,

I'm as giddy as a child in a candy store with a shit ton of money to spend. I went fishing with Raphael yesterday. You know me, always assuming and usually wrong, but I was thinking that he'd have a small fishing boat with a little outboard motor or something, you know, not a yacht but a basic fishing boat. I didn't want him to pick me up because I'm not ready to show him where I live. If it's his intent, I don't want him to think I'm going to be his next candy girl.

I went to meet him down at the marina, driving the yellow Subaru instead of the Mercedes, and I made sure that I got there early. I was sitting in the parking lot listening to some Lana DelRay; she's amazing and that voice, so good. So, where was I?

I was sitting there jamming to my tunes and watching these pickup trucks with these big burly manly men fishermen types pull up. They'd unload their boat into the water and then go park. A few of them had a woman with them, but most just carried a big cooler of, I'm assuming here, beer or alcoholic beverages of choice. It's a gorgeous day out, and it's now almost nine am, the time I'm supposed to meet him. I get out of my car and walk around down by the water, looking for manatees or fish, killing time.

I hear a horn beep, and then I hear it again, and I look up and here's Raphael in this brand-new Chevy pickup. He's got this beautiful aqua boat on a trailer with the name of "What A Catch" painted across the side in a pretty font; a fishing line and hook was painted underlining the words. He waves and then smiles at me from the open window. This big happy, sparkling white teeth everywhere smile, and I'm relieved that the boat is not a small dinghy at all but this big juicy boat with room for at least six or more. I move out of the way, and he backs it down into the water effortlessly. I can't even parallel park, and this man moves his machine like a maestro. He ties it to the dock and tells me he'll be right back.

I watch as he drives away to park. He pulls some things out of the back seat and walks towards me carrying a small cooler, a bag, and a small green tree. He told me it was okay to hop aboard, and he sets his things down and takes my hand as I heave my leg over the edge and find my footing on the bottom of the boat. He hands me the items, unties the boat, and starts the motor. It's so quiet, almost as if it's not running. The boat slides backwards quietly through the water, and then he turns it around and heads out towards the jetty.

Once we made it past the jetty, he showed me where the life preservers were, and I'm thinking that I hope we don't need them, but it's good information to know. I asked him about the tree, and he said it was for me.

"It's a Pachira Aquatica, but most people call it a money tree. They are considered good luck back home, although with the hurricane, I don't know how lucky they were. I didn't want to get you flowers, because everyone buys a beautiful lady flowers, and I guess it's my way of saying I'm sorry again about hooking you yesterday. They're easy to grow, in case you don't have a green thumb and were worried about that," he said, and I was dumbstruck. He told me he didn't want to leave it in the truck to die, so he put it in the shade under the canopy of the boat. It was a cute little tree that stood about a foot high, and I knew just the place in my sunroom where it would be happy. I thanked him and sat down to relax as he maneuvered the boat to wherever it was that we were going.

The waves were light, and they said on the news that morning that it was going to be a good day for boating, no rain in the forecast, and I was looking forward to doing some more fishing. I find it's only fun if you catch something, though, so if nothing else, I could catch a tan.

I had brought a book with me that I had picked up in town, and I was enjoying it and eager to read more, but what I really wanted to do was to talk to him some more, find out who he was and just get to know him better. I let his beautiful lady comment pass without acknowledging it, but for some reason, it made me feel special. I hadn't been called beautiful in years, and coming from such a fine piece of amazingness that he was, I was flattered.

I knocked away the thoughts that were always circling like sharks in my head: he wants something, he'll use you, and it's a lie. He's too pretty, and that's a rule you learned a long time ago. Never trust the pretty boys; they'll break your heart every single time. Not to mention the boat name, was it a fishing play on words or is he a player? I suppose I was going to find out, being his captive first mate all day.

I told the angel/devil on my shoulder to shut the hell up, and I must have said it out loud because he leaned over and said, "What?" I told him, "Nothing," and leaned back in the seat. My sunglasses were blocking the glare from the sun on the water, and I jumped up when I saw something out on a wave bobbing around. It was a sea turtle, and Raphael throttled the boat down and circled back so that I could see it up close. It was watching us, its small beady little eyes filled with curiosity. I laughed and grabbed my phone to get a picture, and it went under but then came right back up again. I managed to get a few good shots before we resumed travel to our destination. I'll send them to Leila; she'll appreciate it.

Raphael was in a swimsuit, and I had one on under my sundress. He asked me if I had ever gone snorkeling, and when I thought back to it, I realized I hadn't. How can a woman profess to be a mermaid, yet never go out to a reef to snorkel? He got up and pulled some equipment from beneath a seat in the back, two sets of fins, face masks, and breathing tubes. He asked me if I was game, and I said sure, only if he promised there wouldn't be any sharks. He laughed loudly. It was a sound that reminded you of a happy song, and he told me that it was the ocean and that anything could be down below. We hadn't started fishing yet, so the water had no blood in it to attract them. When he said that, I was laughing to myself in my head. If there was no more mother nature, there would never be blood in the water, ever again, I thought with an evil chuckle. He promised he'd stay close by me and wouldn't let anything happen. He also had an underwater camera that he put in a mesh pouch that he snapped around his waist.

He maneuvered the boat down off the shore of Caspersen beach and threw out the anchor. He taught me how to gear up and then added a small harpoon gun to his waistband, just in case, he said. I felt better knowing that he could ward off a shark and felt calmer as my body relaxed. The water was that beautiful blue-green color, and we went overboard and into the water. The waves were very light, and I watched as he dunked his mask into the water and then brought it up to seal it around his face. I followed suit and noticed the glass immediately started steaming up from breathing out of my nose. I rinsed it again and put the hose in my mouth and followed as he went down into the water.

The bottom looked smooth, and I held my breath as I gazed around; that's me, always checking for sharks. He smiled at me and touched my arm, gesturing at me to follow him. He went down a few feet and felt around with his hands. As he found a really dark sand patch, he pulled up a rock. He surfaced back up, and I followed. I was having no problem breathing and holding it, and when we came up, he held up a huge shark's tooth in his hand. I couldn't believe the size of it and that it was down there in this water.

I pulled out my tube and asked where the rest of the shark was, and he laughed at me. The next time I swam down as far as he did, and we combed around for more teeth, finding a few but none as large as the one he had found. After a while, I was getting tired, and we moved back to the boat. We had drifted out a little, so we had a short swim to get there. He helped me aboard, and I gave him back the equipment. He started the boat back up, and we went on to fish.

I caught a few fish. One Snook, a Cobia, and a Blue fish. We threw the Snook back but took the rest. He caught a Grouper, but it wasn't big enough, so that ugly sucker went back too. He opened the cooler and handed me an iced tea. He took one too, and I was impressed to see not one single beer in his cooler. He saw me looking and asked if I wanted something besides the tea; he had water, too. I told him I thought most fishermen sat out and drank beer all day. He looked at me and shook his head no; he never drank when he was on the water. He took boating responsibly, and if others wanted to imbibe, then he was cool with that, but he wasn't joining in. It just wasn't worth taking the chance.

I'm thinking wow, sensible and cute. He's like a package of goodness. I just wish I was younger. I asked him how old he was and was surprised to find out that he was forty-two. With that baby face, I found it very hard to believe, and I told him so. He pulled out his license, and sure enough, he's forty-two. That was my shocker of the day, seriously. So, we drifted for a while once we were done fishing and just laid out there soaking up the sun.

He anchored off shore, and he'd swim for a while then come up and stretch out on his towel. He never pressured me to talk, and I found after some time had passed that I wanted to tell him about myself. He listened, asked questions occasionally, but seemed content just being beside me, enjoying the day together.

I thought for a while, as we fell into that comfortable silence, that when I was younger, this was how Alec and I had been. We never had to talk much; we were just content to exist in each other's orbits. What happened to us? I don't know, and I can't ask him. I know I just have to forgive myself for denying myself the right to be truly happy. We could have had so much more, but Alec was always aiming higher and higher, more prestige in his job, more money, more things, just plain more. I was content just going along for the ride with Leila, never asking for anything for myself, and I think the trade-off ended up being I sold myself for his bill of goods. He was happy because he had me and Leila, and Brett on the side, and I was just floundering around being a good wife and mother. I had never explored being me or sought out what truly brought me joy.

What did I want? What was I really out on this beautiful boat with this stunning man for? The answer came like a butterfly, slowly settling itself down upon my mind. Because it made me happy, and I needed more out of my life, and I wasn't going to watch it all drift by me as I sat on the sidelines.

He was watching me as my mind worked through things, and I smiled at him then I leaned over and kissed him on the cheek and thanked him for allowing me the gift of just being here and being grateful for this moment in time. He touched my cheek and smiled, laid his head back down, and closed his eyes. A sincere "You're welcome" fell from his lips, and I closed my eyes as I lay beside him, feeling the warmth of the sun carry me away. I had made a quiet blissful memory that I could call my own.

We stayed out there for a few hours, sleeping and talking, and then he said it was time to head back. He asked me if I wanted to stop and get a bite to eat, and I said I'd love that. We went down to Grove City past Englewood to a bar called The Lighthouse Grill. He pulled the boat up and tied it up to a dock. He was a gentleman, helping me out of the boat, and I found my legs wobbly, and it took me a minute to get my land legs back. The place was pretty busy, and the waitress said it was going to be about a forty-five-minute wait. He asked me if that was okay, and I said sure.

A band was playing some old southern rock covers, and some elderly ladies were in the open area in front of the band, dancing as if their lives depended on it. It was a fun place, and I asked him if he'd mind if I had a glass of wine. He said not at all, and had he not been boating, he would have joined me. He ordered an iced tea, and I ordered a Pinot Grigio. We found a seat out beyond the dining tables and watched boats moving back and forth in the water. My foot was tapping to the music, and he told me I should get up and dance.

"Nope, I'm not going there. Have you seen those ladies? Everyone is staring at them," I told him and took a sip of my wine. He looked over at the dancers and looked back at me.

"They're having fun and enjoying life. That's what it's all about, you know. The only one staring is you. I never can understand why everyone is so fearful about having a good time and letting themselves go, of having fun. In Rincon, we'd be up there dancing all night long. Dancing is art, it's beautiful, and to move your body to the rhythm is one of the sweetest things in life. It's like appreciating a flower. Yes, you can look at it and it's beautiful, or you can pluck it and give it to someone to make them smile. Dance because you love to honor life and your body. You do it because, when you do it, it becomes you. It is pleasurable, and it's as old as time itself." He looked back at the ladies on the dance floor and smiled so sweetly, sat his glass of tea down, and held out his hand to me.

"What have you got to lose? Fear? Come, I won't let them laugh at you." I don't know what the hell I was thinking, but I set my wine down and followed him to the dance floor. The band switched gears as soon as I made my way through the tables and began to play a slow ballad. The singer had a beautiful voice, and I looked around as Raphael wrapped his arms around my waist and looked at me. The song was from The Eagles, "I Can't Tell You Why." Raphael stared into my eyes and smiled as he moved me around the dance floor as effortlessly as he moved his boat.

I lost track of time when he held me, and I felt my eyes fill up with tears as he held me close. The scent of the salt, suntan lotion, and sea air lingered in my senses, and I just stopped thinking. I let myself go, listening to my body as I moved to the music, each note and beat playing straight through into my being. I felt alive, and I didn't care what anyone thought.

Here I am, this middle-aged woman in the arms of a man who looks young enough to be her son, and I didn't care. I was alive and happy, and it showed. When the song ended, everyone clapped, and Raphael bowed before me, as if to thank me for the dance. I looked around and realized we were the only ones out on the dance floor. He held my hand and led me back to our seats. I picked up my wine and realized I didn't really want it after it all. I was high on life and needed no help in that department. They paged us a few minutes later, and we went to find our table.

The sun began to set, and I asked him if he was worried about driving the boat at night. He'd been driving boats for years and knew this area very well, he said, having learned it by fishing it often.

He was a gentleman and not once did he try anything. I wondered once or twice if something was wrong with him, because after Alec, how could I not? Then I relaxed and just enjoyed the process of becoming friends. Did I want something more? I didn't know. I was still unsure after years of neglect, and I was learning a new game here. I told myself to relax and enjoy the ride, let go of expectations, and just let things move naturally.

I didn't make it home until ten, and I slept like a baby. The sun took its toll, and my body melted into a puddle of loose muscles and tired bones as soon as I hit the bed. It felt good, and I woke content and fresh.

Chapter Sixteen

A new day dawns and the world is my oyster.

I watched the skies bubble up as I sat on the terrace drinking my morning therapy. Coffee has always been my breakfast of champions, and I can't function without it. A shelf cloud was out on the horizon, and my cell was pinging me with endless alerts for lightning strikes. This time of year, it is pretty typical, and I guess I like to live dangerously. If I don't see lightning, I stay out as long as I can. I debated what I wanted to do and decided against the yoga on the beach session. Why tempt fate? I could be doing a downward dog and get zapped. That would certainly make the morning headlines because not much else has been happening that's newsworthy. Once the snowbirds fly the coop, driving becomes easier, and you wonder why, when you hear a siren go off, because they're so far and few between. During season, it seems to sound like a never-ending drone of emergency vehicles. You get numb to it after a while.

I had grabbed the newspaper from the front porch and had taken it out to read but wasn't ready to face the negativity I often found. It was a waste of money most days, but I enjoy the funnies. I think they call it comics now, but when I was young, they were always called the funnies, though there wasn't much that was funny there, either. The world has gotten way too political, but I am enjoying *Pickles*. The old lady and man crack me up. Maybe it's because I'm getting up there in age, forgetful too often, and find the truth of their antics hitting closer to home.

Maybe I'll take a drive today. I don't know. What with the storm coming, hiking the parks will be out. I feel like walking, maybe a quick trip to the beach before the rain comes. No, can't do it, the lightning factor and too much open space to get hit. The mall, I'll go to walk the mall. See, wasn't that easy? I don't know why I have such a hard time making my mind up about things. I guess I'm just bored, and I know today will be nowhere close to the excitement of yesterday with Raphael.

The money tree is sitting by the French doors to the terrace, and it made it through the heat on the boat still intact. Leila called yesterday at some point. Her voice sounded happy on the machine, which is now working again, and I felt bad that I missed it, but I wouldn't trade yesterday for the world. I'm sure she'd be happy for me, and next time she calls, I'll tell her all about it. Not much new, so I guess this is it, sorry.

Hey Kate,

I finally did it, I have mermaid hair. I woke up this morning and told myself I was finally going to do something wild and crazy. I saw a woman at the mall today while I was walking, and she had the most beautiful mane of hair streaked in shades of blues, purples, and pinks. It was stunning. Some women do one or two colors and it looks like they did it at home, on the cheap with a kit. It's not very pretty, but this one was out of this world. I had to stop her and ask who did it, and she told me that she did it herself. She was a beautician, and she does house-calls for a price. I asked what it would be for her to do mine similar to hers, and she told me two hundred. I couldn't resist, and she had an opening this evening, and I jumped at it. She just left, and I absolutely love it.

I think normally I'd be worried about what people think, but as I get older, I'm finding I just don't give a shit anymore. It's about me, not them. Look at me, growing a pair, finally. So now with the new hair, I need to go do some clothes shopping. I'm thinking about some light airy gauze, perhaps. We'll see what I find. It's been forever since I bought myself a new wardrobe, and I'm comfy in lounge clothes, but I want to look good again. These threadbare thrift store clothes won't cut it anymore. I love thrift stores and finding a bargain, even though I have the money to buy high scale. I guess I've always been frugal in that way, a thrift store mermaid at heart. I'll let you know what I find. Talk soon.

Howdy Kate,

Okay, so I did some shopping downtown in the historic district and found some pretty snazzy things. I was determined to wear one of my new outfits right then and there, so I had the girl snip the tags off. It's funny. You change something in your style, and all of a sudden, you see women looking at you as if you're somebody, instead of a nobody. I guess not having a girlfriend to keep me in check all of these years has hindered my growth. Alec didn't care what I wore, except at proper events, and those were far and few between. I was thirsty after trying on a ton of clothes, so I stopped for a drink, snagging an outdoor seat at the Daiquiri Deck. It was nice out, and the place was hopping.

A man came in with this fluffy little doodle-something puppy in a pink stroller, and he sat down at the table next to mine. I began making funny faces as I tried to engage his dog, and he smiled. It's been years since I've had any pets, and I looked at that little adorable fluff ball and saw its big brown eyes and its bright pink bubble-gum colored tongue, and I fell in love. He told me he bred them and asked if maybe I'd want one when he bred her next. I thanked him but declined. If I ever do get a dog, rescue dogs will be my breed of choice because there are just so many dumped and in need of a home.

I ate my salad and drank my iced tea while people watching. There were a lot of groups of women out and about. They were laughing and carrying bags from different shops, and I was almost jealous. I wanted to have a tribe, a fun bunch of broads who spoke their truth while they shopped and enjoyed their life.

I felt like crying. What the hell happened to me? Some days, I don't recognize myself, and rattling around in the house alone sucked. I need more. I need companionship. Maybe a

144

vacation, but where the heck would I go? Would I be comfortable going at it alone? I'd have to ask Hope's opinion. Oh God, there I go again. I can't even make a decision or have one plan crafted by my own head. Alec made all the decisions on things like that. I feel lost and know that something's got to give. If I don't change my attitude, I can't change my life.

The man with the dog got up and left behind a magazine. The waitress cleared his spot, tucked away what seemed to be a hefty tip, and left the magazine there. I leaned over and grabbed it and started aimlessly browsing it for ideas. It was a AAA mag that had a little bit of everything, including a lot of cruises, hmmm...maybe I'd look into that. I live in paradise, but there's so much more out there that I've never seen. There are a lot of workers on board keeping an eye on things, and I've never heard of anyone getting assaulted on one. Pushed overboard by a significant other, yes, but raped and pillaged, no. I don't know. I'm not sure. I'll think on it tonight. I'm in no rush.

I walked through town after lunch and just window shopped. I didn't need anything more, but I wasn't ready to head home just yet. I moved farther down the street where the stores begin to thin out and came to what used to be a really fun gift shop. Mr. and Mrs. Eldridge had run it for what seemed like a hundred years. I had heard that the Mr. passed away last year. He was a fossil when I first moved here, and it's been something like twenty years now, and being newly widowed myself, I knew that the Mrs. must be going through hell.

They were always such a cute couple, very attentive to each other. I never went into that store without coming out with a bag filled with unique items. There was a big going out of business sign across the front of the window glass. The big red letters seemed sad to me, like a final notice of termination. I pushed the door open and went in to see what was left. The shelves were mostly bare, a handful of items moved to the front of the store and settled haphazardly on the rack closest to the door. It was like the land of misfit junk. It was unrecognizable from the last time I'd been in. Mrs. Eldridge sat at the counter. Her eyes looked tired, and a touch of sadness lay there. I knew that look well. She came around and hugged me when I made it past the lonely rack.

"You made it for the final hurrah. Oh, it's so good to see you, my dear. How's it shaking?" Her favorite phrase had always made me smile.

"Shaking it as well as I can, getting warmer and ready for a cool down, but we know well enough that that's not going to happen anytime soon," I said and hugged her back with heartfelt joy. She looked around the store and sighed heavily.

"I'd say I'm gonna miss this place, but I'm ready for a break from it. It's not fun going it alone, and now that Jimmy's gone, I guess my heart just isn't in it. It was a good stretch, forty years here, and we had just had our sixty-fifth anniversary a month before he passed. I'm glad we made it as far as we did. Lot of young folk these days don't have it as good as us, but we were blessed, truly blessed." Her eyes were bright with unshed tears, and I hugged her again. She offered to get me a water, but I declined.

"What are you going to do with the store?" I asked, looking around and realizing the interior was quite darling. There were a lot of little cubbies in the wall, with a few inset shelves, airy rooms that led from one to the other, and the building itself was a small cottage. Something went through me as I stood there. Even though it was bare and sad, knowing how I had always loved shopping there, I knew there was so much potential to the place, and I got this crazy idea that I needed to buy it.

She smiled at me and shook her head. "I was thinking I should rent it out, but I wonder if I really want to be a landlord at my age. We've made a good living here, and we even lived here when we first got married, but I have a home and have no need to be living in the thick of things down here. Besides, I love my garden, and cement isn't the same as flowers and green trees surrounding a living space, and my ocean view, I wouldn't trade that for the world. I guess I'll shut it up for a while until I decide. Why do you ask? You're not interested in it by any chance?"

Her eyes brightened as the possibility flitted through her head like a meandering butterfly, and I don't know what I was thinking, but I looked at her with this stronger than anything I've ever felt conviction in my soul and told her, "I want to buy it."

"I have this vision in my mind of a gift shop filled with seaside things, mermaids, but not cheap shells and things like the other shops seem to carry. I'd like some fun jewelry, books by local authors, and maybe some art by local artisans too. Oh, I can see it in my mind perfectly. I have no idea how to begin, but would you be willing to sell me the shop and give me some guidance on buying and merchandising?"

Sharon looked at me with a twinkle in her eye and laughed. She held me tightly as her body moved back and forth almost like a happy dance, and I think I knew it was going to happen. What the hell was I thinking? I thought to myself, and I smiled.

This wave of steady strength filled me, and I knew it would be perfect, and that's when Destiny's Dream gift shop was born. I didn't need to travel and see the world, because I was content in my world here in Venice and soon to be in my shop. I'd meet new people and have something to occupy my time. I didn't need the money. I just needed something, and I felt that this would be it. Sharon walked over and giggled, locked the door and grabbed me by the hand, and led me to the back room.

There was a small kitchen, and she asked me if I wanted some iced tea, and I said yes. She poured us two tall glasses full and motioned for me to sit at the table. She sat across from me and asked me some questions, gauging my knowledge on running a business and whether or not I could secure a loan for purchase of the building and the contents to fill it. It was a good chunk of change, but I had it just sitting there festering in the bank. Our home was paid off, and I could afford it without hurting myself in any way.

She told me roughly what they had made money-wise each month, and what I would earn would hinge on the value of the goods I carried. We came up with a plan, and I told her that, on Monday, I would sit down with my financial advisor and get hopping on securing what I'd need. She stood up then and walked me through the back rooms. Upstairs was like a loft, and she used it as storage space for excess items, and there were extra fixtures, a mannequin without arms that sat lonely in a corner and startled me for a second when I bumped into it, sending her rocking forward. Sharon chuckled and straightened "Beatrice" back into place. Jimmy had named her years ago, and she was usually clad in aprons and scarves.

148

My mind was moving a hundred miles an hour, and I could see it, freshly painted and new shelving, pretty items that people would pick up and ooh and ahh over, and with a kitchen, maybe I would whip up some mini-cupcakes or cookies for customers to buy and snack on as they shopped. I felt my heart beating, each new scene in my mind escalating my vision, and damn, it felt so right, and I knew it was a good plan. We talked for another hour, and when we made it back to the front of the store, I told her about what I saw in my head, and she nodded in agreement.

"When I watch you, I see myself all those years ago. It's almost like you're where I was and it's been a good life here. The location is perfect for foot traffic, and I know, if it all pans out, you're going to love it. I love the name too, and I know Jimmy is watching and nodding with that sly little smile he had when he was happy. I won't put it on the market yet. You do your thing and let me know how it goes. I'll be happy to show you the ropes, and I'll work on a list of things you'll need. Do you have a computer? We did it all by hand, old school style, but I would think there are a lot easier ways nowadays. Call me later this week, and we'll come up with a plan. You'll want to get ordering bags and things if you want your store name on them. That takes some time. We can get together and go through and look at some sites for inventory, but if you want local art, you might want to put an ad out. You'll get some mileage out of that, but you'll get some crackpots too, so be prepared."

I was taking notes in my little notepad, and I got her phone number, prices for the store and fixtures, and roughly what she paid in taxes every year on the property. I would have to get an inspector; she insisted on that, because she'd fix anything needed before I took over ownership. I was elated, and I knew today was the first day of an exciting new chapter in my life. I couldn't wait. I would be a gift store owner, and I knew I'd succeed.

I've always believed that things happen for a reason, and had I not been down there to stop in on Sharon's last hurrah, I never would have thought of buying a cottage or running my own store. It was going to be perfect, and it would be all mine. I wanted to share the news with someone, so I called Leila, but it went right to voicemail. I told her to call me when she found time, and I drove down to sit on the beach for a while.

I sat down on my blanket that I kept in the trunk and tried to calm my excited mind and meditate on the possibilities, which to me were endless. The waves were small, and there were a few people down there, some swimmers, walkers and fishermen. I recognized the form of Raphael a hundred feet away, and I stood up and walked down to talk to him. He smiled when he saw me coming and waved.

He had a fresh haircut. The thin line of salt and pepper at his temples made me smile, and I wondered why I had not noticed it before. He listened while I told him about the shop, and by the time I was done, he seemed very excited for me. He offered to help me in any way that he could. Work was slowing down for him because the season was over, and he had more time on his hands. He cast out again, and within moments, he got a bite on the line. He handed me the pole, and I got to pull in a snapper. It put up a fight, and it felt good, the feel of my muscles working as the fish fought the line. He got his net and pulled it out, standing waist deep in the water as I watched him work with the fish, unhooking it and setting it free only after holding it up for me to see.

The man was beautiful, I thought to myself, and I watched him as he strode out of the waves, his swim shorts clinging to his muscular body. I was feeling things stir up in me, things I hadn't felt in what seemed like years. I wanted him in a primal way, and I didn't know if it was the excitement of my day or just a yearning for human contact. He smiled at me, and I blushed. I know, he's not a mind reader, but I felt like my feelings were etched across my face. He asked me if I wanted to go out for a cocktail at the deck, and I said yes. He packed up his gear and followed me over to my blanket. He helped me fold it up, and we walked back to the parking lot, chatting about his week at work, and I felt good just being with him.

I followed him back to the district, parked over in Centennial park close to the bathrooms where he went in to change out of his dripping-wet suit then walked over to "The Deck." The singer was crooning a Jimmy Buffet ballad, and there were a few people sitting in groups chatting while they watched. His guitar skills were pretty good, and there was a big fishbowl close to the area where he sat. A sign marked "tips appreciated" was written on a purple sticky note that was attached to the edge of the bowl. The bowl was half-filled with bills and change and no goldfish.

We took a seat on the other side of the building where we could talk and not feel like we were interrupting his act. Raphael was relaxed and said he'd spent the morning with friends then went fishing. It was nice being around him, and I sat back and listened to him talk about his day. He loved my plan of opening a gift shop, and the more I explained about each room and what I had in mind, he formulated ideas for building in some new shelving and wood details for a comfy decorator effect. I liked the idea of a sharp white with turquoise accents, thinking with

151

my love of all things mermaid, I could then easily incorporate pinks, greens, and lavenders to finish it. I couldn't wait to get started, but until Monday, there wasn't much I could do.

Raphael had a few suggestions and seemed eager to be a part of my new project, and I realized how much I appreciated the fact that he had found me by accident yet chose to stay because of a genuine fondness. I felt worthy, and I think my attitude was showing. Confidence is always hard to come by, unless you were raised in an environment where it oozed from your entire family like sweat on a September day in south Florida. I wasn't gifted with it, but it was coming slowly but surely.

I asked him what his goals were and if he was going to live at his sister's house long term, and he was quite honest with me. I never asked about how he could afford the new pickup and the juicy boat, so I guess in that way I was stereotyping him. Shame on me for that, but not having a lot of people around who weren't upper echelon moneyed doctor types and such, you get a bit set in your ways. It doesn't make it right, and I'm certainly not making excuses for myself. I'm just saying it's something that I needed to work on.

He had told me how he had worked in the hospitality industry in Puerto Rico when we were out on the boat, but what I had not known was that he had a huge place right on the ocean. It was a multitude of suites that he rented out to the wealthy. He had made $2300 per week for one suite, in one building alone where he had ten of them, five with ocean front views. After the hurricane, the island was in complete devastation, and he didn't go into details, but I get the sense that he lost someone near and dear to him. I will wait until he's ready to talk about it, but he told me that he decided to come to the states after that. Until he knows where he wants to be permanently, he's holding off on buying.

He sold off a few of his buildings but has a property manager overseeing the rest. Again, never assume, and you can't judge a book by its cover. He probably has more money than me, and here I'm worried about inviting him into my home. I know, you're thinking, do a background check just to make sure, and the side of me that has the hard time trusting knows this. I just would like to believe again in my perceptions and take the chance that, this time, I could be right. Time will tell, of course, but I just thought I'd give you the highlights of my latest endeavor. I'm so proud of myself, and I hope you are too.

Chapter Seventeen

Destiny's dream becomes a reality...not a reality show.

Well, it's been a whirlwind. Three and a half months later and I'm exhausted yet exhilarated. I was able to close on the store, and now it's getting closer to opening day. Only a few more weeks and I should be ready for the unveiling. Raphael is a Godsend, and I am thankful that he's becoming such an integral part of my life. I've been working non-stop, and the place is shaping up nicely. The items I've ordered are here, and I have them stored in a shipping Pod behind the shop. The walls are painted, and a new roof will go on next week, compliments of Sharon and the inspection, and it should be complete by opening day.

Oh, I finally heard from Harmony. I know I don't mention her much, but that's because she kind of lives off the grid now in Montana. She married a guy named Dwayne, and they're both heavily into ranching. They have cattle, horses, goats, and God only knows what else. They have six kids, and she doesn't travel; there's always too much to do with the ranch. I was always a little jealous each time a new baby was born. It seemed like she was churning them out as fast as a rabbit. She did name one of the girls Destiny, so I have a namesake.

I guess you could say we're kind of estranged. I didn't care for her choice of a husband; he always struck me as bossy and domineering, truth be told. She's happy though, and I guess that's all that matters. I can count on her each Christmas sending me a gift basket of goat milk products. She makes them herself and sells them down in their little town at the farmers market. She took her hippie-sounding name and is living the lifestyle she wants. I guess I equate a life off the grid to the communes of the sixties, peace, love and goat milk, baby.

What else, hmm...Raphael made these darling little shelves and put in some new inset lighting, and I know, once it's all filled, it's going to be amazing. I stocked the kitchen with some bakeware, and I'm going to make a ton of cookies for the opening event. I will freeze a bunch so that I make sure I have enough. Other than that, I guess not much new.

Hey Kate,

Sorry again, but I've been busy. It's now October, and the snowbird season will be upon me shortly. I've already seen some RV's rolling their way into town. They're behemoths lumbering slowly red light to red light. It's as bad as being stuck behind a bus, but at least with a bus, I know where the signs are, and then I can anticipate where they'll stop.

I want to make sure I'm ready for the crush of happy souls from the North, eager to embrace the warmth and hospitality my adopted state affords. Traffic is going to be a bitch, but my house is close enough that I can ride my bike every day and not have to take up a space with my car. It's important to me that I make good use of my parking lot; it's pretty small.

Leila is in Spain right now, and she's so excited for the store to succeed. She's not sure if she'll make it home for Christmas, and it sounds like she has a love interest now. She didn't say much, but I can tell that she's growing up and learning a lot out on the road. I wished her my best and sent her much love as I always do. She's still doing well financially, minding her P's and Q's, so I don't have to worry about her draining me by living beyond her means. I did well with my girl, and I'm so proud that she's living her life on her own terms. I'm proud that I'm living mine now, too.

I have ten different artists' work that will be on the walls of the shop. I get a hefty commission on each piece they sell, and their work is magnificent. I handpicked the cream of the crop, and it's going to make the shop come alive with all that beauty. There are also five different local authors as of now, whose work will be showcased in a special section just for them. The rest of the goods are candles, glass pieces, handmade jewelry, and a hodgepodge of this and that. I've selected pieces that are not sold anywhere else on the island. I went store by store in town and made sure that I'm not carrying anything that's already out there. I've got to stay fresh and unique, and if I find something later that's being sold by a competitor, then I won't carry it any longer. My vendors know how I feel about it, and if all goes well, it will fall perfectly into place without having to find new ones.

I went with the crisp white and turquoise color scheme, and I now also have a mermaid painted on the wall right when you come in. Of course, she is complete with mermaid hair. No, I won't have to paint over it either. It made me laugh out loud when the woman finished it, as it reminded me of my childhood all over again. I told her the story so that she would know I wasn't laughing at her work.

Raphael has been spending more time with me. Nothing romantic has happened between us yet, because by the time we're done working on the store, we go out to eat out of necessity, and we're drained physically. He did kiss me goodnight the other evening, and I could barely sleep. My brain wouldn't stop thinking of him, and I will have to make a decision on where I want this to go. He isn't pushing me, and I'm not making any advancements towards him. Perhaps we're both wary of anything deeper. He's got to go to Puerto Rico this weekend and check on things with his properties, and he asked me to come along. He knew that, with the store opening soon, I wouldn't be able to make it this trip, but maybe next time. He says he tries to go there every three to four months or so.

Depending on how it goes with the store, I know that I will need some help at some point, especially during season. A really sweet woman named Bonnie stopped by when we were painting the walls. We had the door open to vent the smell, and she asked if she could peek around. I told her it would be fine. She's around seventy-five or so, and her husband's been gone for over

157

twenty years. She offered to help out with the store if I ever find I need someone. She's very spry for her age. She had her own business years ago and is just looking for part time, maybe just a few days a week, something to fill her time. I suppose it is better to hire someone who is older and with more experience, and I think they would have a better work ethic than someone younger.

I see the kids these days, and they're attached to their phones. How can you walk down the street if you can't even look up? It drives me batty, and I'm glad Leila isn't anything like that. I may hire Bonnie when the time comes, but I'm not quite that far yet. I have her number just in case.

I am having a sign made for the shop by a place down the street. I designed it myself, and it will be ready this weekend. They offered to hang it for me, but I'll wait until Raphael gets back. He's a pro at things like that, and he's enjoying being a part of it all. The tables and some other fixtures will be in early next week, and then I can start unpacking the boxes. I've got it all figured out price-wise, and I bought a new Mac to be able to order, but the most unique thing I just had to have, is one I found at an antique shop. It's an old sea-foam green-colored register, and I may use it, but for now I enjoy just staring at it and pushing the buttons, hearing the little bell when the drawer pops open. It works perfectly, but with the credit card aspect, I'll have to run those separately. I've already got the equipment for that ready to go, and I ran a charge on my card and then refunded myself just to make sure I knew how it worked. I'm feeling so smart.

Oh, and before I go, I stepped on the scale this morning and clocked in at 137 pounds. Damn, if that doesn't make my day, nothing will. Woo Hoo! All this work on the store is toning me up nicely. I'm proud of my body and of this store. Life is good. Maybe when I get a moment, I'll hop down to get a milkshake to treat myself. We'll see. God knows I'm working my calories off daily, so just one little shake won't hurt.

Hey Kate,

I'm sorry I haven't been talking much. It gets pretty busy here, and with only one week until opening, it still seems like there's still so much to do. Raphael got back, and I realized how much I missed him, and I think he missed me too. I feel like the last few months are almost surreal, and I woke the other night in a cold sweat.

Someone told me once when I was younger that, if you're dreaming and you die in that dream, it scares you literally to death. As in, you don't wake up and you die right then and there while you're sleeping.

I laughed it off because I had a dream that I was pushed out of a second story window by a boy I liked. I fell backwards, smashing through the glass and landing on the concrete below, breaking my body, my neck and back. I died and came back to haunt the boy for the rest of his life, through high school and into his adulthood. Needless to say, I woke up the next morning bright-eyed and bushy-tailed and very much alive. Of course, I find out a few days later that my boy crush is now dating my best friend. Maybe my dreams have seemed to me almost like a harbinger of some kind of bad news.

Last night, I had a horrible dream. I don't have them very often, but when I do, they are wild and unnerving. In the dream,

159

Raphael and I were swimming, and a current sucked me out into the Gulf. I screamed for help, and I could feel myself going under. I'd surface, searching for him, and he was trying to help me, but he never got far enough out to reach me. I finally couldn't take the strength of the waves and the endless pull, and I began to sink, exhausted and swallowing water as I drowned in my beautiful blue ocean. I could see the world around me and felt my life flash before my eyes, then I awoke in a cold sweat, dripping wet and crying. I couldn't catch my breath, and I was afraid. Of what, I don't know.

It was almost like having an anxiety attack, and I know this because I used to have them after Leila and Liam were born. I was always so scared of losing baby girl, hence the psychiatrist and the need to be engaged with talking to you. It has helped, don't get me wrong, but I'm in unfamiliar territory with the store, and as time ticks by and the opening gets closer, I'm finding myself frazzled. Maybe some meditation is in order again. I'll try it and let you know, but in the meantime, I'm going to go bake some more cookies, and I can't multitask with both you and my cookie creations. But the sweet confections are coming out beautifully. So, meditation podcast and cookies it will be, bye Kate.

Hey Kate,

Now I've done it. My reality has turned into a reality show. I was baking cookies last night, and the recipe called for melted chocolate. Easy peasy, I know, right? So, I had my double boiler pan on the stove filled with chocolate chunks melting down, my temperature gage was immersed in the thick sweet chocolate, and I was watching it closely so I didn't scald it. The radio was on, and I was listening to sounds of the 70's and then my all-time favorite song "Dancing Queen" from ABBA came on. I was on a roll. I had the cookies waiting for the chocolate drizzle, and Raphael was on his way over. I was dancing a little bit, not too much mind you, and somehow the sleeve of my house dress caught the handle of the pan and it pulled it right off the stove and down my front. I screamed and held the material away from me so that I didn't get burned and then carefully pried my dress off over my head. I didn't want to burn my face, and I'm screaming like a banshee, and of course, Raphael arrives at that very moment. He comes running in like the house is on fire.

I'm standing in the kitchen quivering from my close call with a burn unit, and Raphael is staring at me. It took me a minute for my brain to register that I had no bra on, my pink and white polka-dotted panties, and now no house dress. The only thing handy to cover up with was a dish towel, and that wasn't going to cover much. I turned red and looked at him as his mouth opened and closed. He looked like a fish let off of the hook, and I didn't know what to say. He realized I was embarrassed and turned around while I slipped out of the room and upstairs to change into something, anything.

When I came back downstairs, I found that he had picked up my dress and had cleaned up the chocolate on the floor. He was leaning on the counter and snacking on a cookie. He asked me if I needed him to go out to buy more chocolate. I'm thinking, wow, here I am standing before him half-naked, and he tidied up after me. Perhaps he's just polite that way, but I think it would have been nice for him to make a move, maybe? I don't know. Granted, I was still startled at having almost burned myself with the boiling chocolate, and a nice guy wouldn't take advantage, right?

Grrr...I don't know. I'll ask him. I won't know unless I ask, and neither of us are mind readers. Perhaps, had he gotten there earlier and had seen the dance, he'd be more willing to make a move. Who knows? I just know this not-quite dating thing is a bite in the ass, and I'm too busy and not getting any younger.

I guess I do want something more between us. I hope he feels the same way. Maybe I will just put it out of my head until after the store gets settled. I'm busy enough these days, but when he's building a shelf or painting, I just watch him and feel this heavy ache. When we are together, there's no place I'd rather be than with him. He leaves me feeling peaceful, like I'm grounded and in line with something higher. I've never felt that with anyone, ever, and it's, I don't know, kind of close to amazing.

Hey Kate,

I don't know how long my eyes will stay open, but I'm so keyed up, and I figure that by talking to you, it will slow my mind down. We opened the store today, and the event was spectacular. At least a hundred or more people showed up to check us out, and sales were brisk from the moment we opened until we closed the door. I love this town so much because of the nature of the people. They are so wonderful for shopping local and supporting us small businesses.

I believe my little place is fitting right in perfectly. I received a ton of compliments on the bright happy colors and the shelving additions and alcoves we've added, and when everyone was finally gone at closing time, I just stood there enjoying the quiet and meditating over the day. I see a great future for

Destiny's Dream. I've got to go to sleep now my friend. I'm whipped, so, nighty night.

Good morning Kate,

I slept like a baby. I close the store on Sundays as there's not much action down here, and hey, even I need a day off. Raphael and I are going out on the boat today to do some fishing and just to relax and recharge. He was such a blessing yesterday with the grand opening, charming the ladies, and he's an amazing salesman. I may have to keep him. After all, he is cute as a button.

Chapter Eighteen

Frogs, and snails, and puppy dog tails.

So, where do I begin? It's been six months since Destiny's Dream opened, and it's been incredible. Running a business is tough work, more so during season, but at least when I go to sleep at night, I know that I've done the best I could. I think I'm mastering it without too many issues cropping up. I hired Bonnie, and she's working out very well. She's got a lot of friends, and many of them stop down to see her and shop, and if it's a slow day, I can skip out, leave her in charge, and go to lunch with Raphael. I stay close by, but it gives me a break to recharge my batteries.

Things are going well with him, and he spends a lot of time at my home when he can. I've thought about asking him to move in, but something is keeping me from asking. He's starting his own business now, at least during season. He's going to be using his boat as a charter for fishermen. He'll be taking them out for most of the day; this way, he can fish and make money too. There seems to be a high demand for that down here, and his rates are reasonable. It pays more than the Siesta Key job, and he's his own boss. He's done by six most nights, but he has to be at the marina by five a.m. I'm glad he's got his own interests. I can't see him a lot of the time because of the shop, but he does stop in and help out occasionally. Nothing gets a purse open like an energetic, young-stud smiling at you and doling out compliments like Halloween candy to trick-or-treaters. I don't encourage him, but the ladies love him, and when he's not in, I hear all the women asking where he is. I guess sometimes I'm just chopped liver, ha, but I'll take it. He's all mine, and I trust him.

Leila is coming back home. Apparently, Julia fell somewhere on their trip while in Spain. She broke her leg and needs to recoup before they head on to the next destination. They decided to come back stateside in case she needs surgery. It didn't sound like the hospitals over there are very good, and she wants to make sure she gets the best care possible. I am so excited. It's been much too long since I've held my baby girl, and I can't wait to see how she likes the shop. Julia is going to be staying here with us. Her parents are divorced, and no one's ever home to help her, so Leila is playing nursemaid to her. She's always good that way. Julia is lucky to have such a good friend.

I told her a little about Raphael and our relationship because he's been around more often, and I didn't want her to think that I'm being promiscuous. I would never do such a thing, hmmm...

I told him about Leila returning from Spain and that I had told her about us. He finally told me about his life in Puerto Rico and the reason he came here. I thought my life was tragic, but I think his story has mine beat.

He was engaged to a woman named Malia, and they had a child together, a six-year-old boy named Gabriel. They were getting away from the coast to hunker down up in the forest at a friend's home. The house in the hills was reinforced for hurricanes. Raphael was back down on the coast buttoning up the properties in anticipation of the coming storm, and he told me their car went off of the road. Malia had come around a curve, and she swerved to miss a dog that was standing in the road; their car overturned. I guess the roads up in the mountains are really narrow and treacherous on a good day. He lost them both and hadn't wanted to talk about it until he was ready. They're buried on the island, but he didn't want to be around for the constant reminders. That's when he headed here.

He looked so sad, and I knew how he was feeling, having lost both a child and a husband. I just held him tightly, and then we sat there in the dying light on the terrace. He kissed me then, and I mean, really kissed me. He said that he was ready to move on with his life, to leave the past behind and let it go. He was ready for more than just friendship, and I told him that we had the rest of our lives to live. I was laying no claim on him; things had been going well, and I was busy with the shop, but I knew I really cared for him, and that if I was who he wanted his future to be with, then I was on board with that. I trusted him, and now that I knew his secret, there was nothing stopping us.

He spent the night, and I woke up crying at one point, wishing that Alec could have been more like him, loving and passionate and present. I don't know why I thought of Alec; he hadn't been in my thoughts for what seemed like forever. I had put that part of my life behind me. It was gone, done and buried. But with Raphael, he was very attentive to my needs and I to his. They were like apples and oranges if I had to compare the two men of my life.

We finally lay down to sleep around three a.m. It was nice waking up wrapped in his arms, his face soft and relaxed in the pre-dawn light. I slipped out of bed and went down and swam in the pool naked. I lay on my back and floated as the sun lay just below the horizon. The dawn was peaceful and quiet, and I listened to the sound of the beating of my heart beneath the water, and I just relaxed. I had no thoughts in my mind. I was just calm, and I touched my breasts and my stomach and smiled. I was where I wanted to be, and it felt like I'd come full circle in a way, complete and whole once more.

I heard a noise and looked up as Raphael was stepping down into the pool. He was as beautiful and as naked as I was, and I watched him as he moved through the water, closer and closer to where I was treading water. I could feel my heart as it began beating harder, and he closed the distance and took me in his arms. I was his mermaid, and his mouth covered mine, then his lips moved down my neck, and I leaned my head back as his he licked my breast. I felt so alive, and I smiled as I watched his face. His eyes were as deep as my beloved sea, and they stared into mine with a look of unabashed need, and I knew then that this was what love was, to be held and cherished and wanted, and to feel the same way within yourself for another.

The sun was reaching up to the edges of the trees, and I heard a car door slam. I looked at Raphael and asked him what day it was. He told me Monday, and I realized that the landscaping and lawn maintenance workers were here to do the yard. He laughed at me.

"Are you serious?" he said, and I nodded. I began quick-stepping to get out of the pool before the crew made it around to the back of the house. I had just wrapped a bath sheet around my body when John, the head gardener, strode around the hedge. He stopped dead in his tracks, and Raphael was still waist-deep in the water looking at me with a grin on his face. I stepped between John and the pool and held out a towel to Raphael, and he stepped out of the pool and wrapped it around his waist.

John cleared his throat and smiled at the two of us, apologizing profusely, and then he turned and walked away, saying they'd start in the front. I laughed as Raphael wrapped me tight in his arms, threatening to finish what we'd started, but I told him it was best not to scare off the guys. They were very good at what they did, and I didn't want to look for a new grounds crew. We went into the house, and I clicked on the coffee to brew, and then went upstairs to shower before getting ready for work. Raphael joined me in the shower, and by the time we finished, I felt rushed to get to the store. I owned the place, and if I opened a few minutes late, it wasn't going to hurt anything, especially on a Monday.

When I got to work, there were three ladies sitting out on the front bench waiting for me to open. I unlocked the door and let them browse while I finished setting up for the day, putting out a big plate of salted caramel shortbread cookies and fussing with a display. One of the women mentioned that that was why they had stopped at my place first. A sweet treat before a full day of shopping, and I knew then that the cookie idea was a hit. I vowed to continue the new tradition.

I made a different kind of cookie daily and had a stockpile frozen, just in case I couldn't get to it. I made a few dozen, but once they were gone, then that was it, so everyone knew to get there early or miss out. Word had gotten out, and I could always depend on seeing some happy faces waiting for me. The early bird gets the worm, and ninety percent of the time, they bought something at the store, which made it worth it. Sugar and all good things, done Destiny's way.

Leila is due in tonight, and I have to go pick her up at the airport around seven. Raphael is taking the night off and going out with friends. It will give me time to reconnect with Leila. I'm excited and can't wait to see her beautiful face. I missed my baby girl something fierce. I set up a room for Julia last night and put fresh flowers from the garden in both rooms. Well, I may not get to talk to you much for the next few days, so I'll let you go. I just wanted you to know that life rocks and that everything is going super-duper excellent.

Hi again Kate,

So, there's apparently a whole lot of news going on. Leila's flight made it in a little early, and by the time I arrived, she and Julia had their bags and apparently a new puppy they rescued over there. He's a cute little brown and black terrier, and he's been all vetted and fixed. His name is Max, and he looks a little like the dog from the old holiday show, *How The Grinch Stole Christmas*. She told me that he's almost fully housebroken and that she'd make sure to take care of everything. She knows that I'm not home much with the shop.

Julia looked like she's in a bit of pain, and I pulled up and then helped Leila load up their gear. They both sat in the back seat and held Max. He was a curious little thing, but I didn't want him to pee in the Mercedes. It was only thirty minutes or so to get home, and he did his business on a grassy spot before we left, so that made me feel better.

I haven't had a dog around in ages, and he has a high-pitched yipping little bark; being so young, he hasn't found his deep doggy voice yet. He is cute though, and I can see why she brought him home. I'm not sure how she's going to travel with a dog once they are back on their feet, and for some reason, I can see Max becoming a permanent fixture here. Don't ask me how; I'm just a parent, and I can tell when my child is up to something.

So, the girls talked about their trip all the way home, telling me about Peru, Ireland, and about the trail in Spain. They met a lot of nice folks and then explained how Julia had had the accident. Apparently, it was caused by falling down a flight of stairs at the hostel they were lodging at. The lighting was poor or pretty much non-existent, and she had slipped. Thank God it wasn't while they were out in the boonies, because there'd have been no one to help them out there.

We got back to the house, and I ordered some pizza and a salad to be delivered, and Leila hauled their stuff up the stairs to their rooms. Max ran around the house, his little feet slipping and sliding on the cool tile, and he reminded me almost of Leila as a child, the way she'd wear her slippers and slide across the floor pretending she was an ice-skater. He came over and sat down beside me, unsure what to do about the stairs. I pet him and talked to him like a little baby. He'd tip his head this way and that, staring at me with those big brown puppy eyes, and my heart melted right then and there.

It was going to be a tough go for Julia getting up the stairs, but they told me not to worry. She'd wear shoes so that she didn't slip on the tile, or she would be bare-footed, no socks. Once they were settled, we sat out on the terrace at the table, waiting for the food to arrive.

Max was running in and out of the chair legs, and I asked them where they found him. Apparently, he adopted them out on their trek. He was hungry, and it was unusually cold one night when they pitched their tent, and he had been following them. They didn't exactly want a dog but knew that they couldn't leave him out there alone to die, so they made a make-shift leash out of a cord and brought him along. He was around six months old now, and the vet told them that he wouldn't get much bigger. He filled out as they fed him better food, and they became inseparable. I expressed my fear of how they'd be able to take him back with them when they left and traveled more. Leila looked sort of guilty then and told me she thought a little dog would be perfect for me, what with Alec being gone and her traveling so much. Ah hah! I knew it.

So, Max would end up being mine. I laughed, and he came running over to me, wanting to be picked up. I had him on my lap when the doorbell rang, and Leila went to get the food. Max licked my face, and his little tongue was hanging out through his little bristly face, and I could have sworn he had a look on his face like he knew I was his new mom.

Leila brought out some plates and silverware, the pizza, and the antipasto salad. I realized I hadn't eaten since lunch, and I was hungry. I let the girls grab what they wanted, and I sat there feeling calm and easy. I set Max down and chewed on my cheesy pepperoni slice as the sun slipped down to touch the horizon. The girls ate happily, and I looked up at one point and saw the way they were with each other. There's a certain way that people look when they have deeper feelings for each other, and I wondered for a moment if the relationship Leila was in was with Julia. Mother senses kick in that way.

We chatted for a little while as we finished the food, then I took Max out into the yard to do his thing. I made a mental note to myself to let the landscaping service know about him so that they don't leave the gate open and watch for tootsie rolls hidden in the lawn. Nothing worse than dog crap wedged into your shoes, falling out of the tread like crusty stinky waffles. Our yard was fenced, but things can happen. Now that I had Max, I didn't need the anxiety of worrying about him escaping or running away. We had coyotes and bobcats on the island, and the idea of Max becoming something's dinner made my blood run cold.

He chased the little lizards that ran around but wasn't very skilled at catching them, thank God. I'd hate to be having to pick up dog barf constantly. He gave up after a while, and we retired for the night. I had to work in the morning, and Leila told me that I could sleep with Max if I wanted to; she wouldn't mind. Max looked at me with his head cocked at that little angle, and I picked him up and carried him up the stairs. I sat him down at the top in the hallway, and he had the choice of going with the girls or coming with me, and after a moment of considering his options, he actually followed me into my room. I was happy about that, and I closed the door. He sat down next to the bed, waiting patiently to be picked up and added to the plentiful pillow collection.

I slept for a few hours and woke up having to go to the bathroom. Max was crashed out next to me and didn't budge when I slid out of bed. I went in to the hallway and saw Julia's door open. The lights were out and I peeked in, concerned that she might need something, and I saw that her bed was empty. It was then that my suspicions were confirmed. My daughter was having an affair with her friend Julia. I stood there for a minute and took a few deep breaths. How did I feel about it? How was I supposed to feel about it? At my age, not much shocks me anymore, and I had had a feeling, but I think this cemented the truth. Whoa. I will have to meditate on this.

I tiptoed back to bed and lay there in the dark. I stroked Max's bristly fur as his little legs moved quickly; apparently, he was deep in the throes of a puppy dream. He whimpered lightly and then settled. I thought about Leila and Julia. I couldn't change anything, and I certainly couldn't tell her how to live her life and who she should and shouldn't love. I think I was just sad when I realized that this may mean I'd never have grandchildren. I didn't want to assume and knew in the morning or at some point I'd hear it from their mouths. I'd wait for her to tell me what was up. I'll be supportive of whatever path she chooses to take with her life.

I felt a little sad, yet so mature. I had enough love in my heart to allow my daughter to be who she wanted. If she was gay, then so be it. I wouldn't love her any less, and I would welcome Julia with open arms. I snuggled back beneath the blankets and pressed my face up against Max's warm little body. He whimpered once, and I fell asleep content with my decisions, smelling the scent of his doggy shampoo as my face was nestled into his fur. I have found that life liked to do the tango with me, twisting and turning like a sensual dance, but beautiful in all its elegance and grace.

I was blessed, and I knew it. I had my daughter, and now Julia, beneath my roof, and a new snuggle buddy. I hoped Raphael liked dogs and knew I'd soon find out.

Chapter Nineteen

Eyes wide closed...new days of lessons learned.

I woke to a cold wet nose sniffing my face. I opened my eyes and blinked to focus and check the clock. Max saw that I was awake and began nudging me. It was still dark, but the clock was showing five a.m. I figured he had to go outside and do his business, so I threw on a bathrobe and my slippers and turned to find that he'd curled back up in the warm spot I had just vacated. His little eyes were sleepy. He yawned and then laid his head down on my pillow. I scooped him up, because if I'm going to get up, he's going to get up. It was his idea after all.

I carried him down the stairs and grabbed a flashlight, headed out to the terrace, and shone the light on the yard, searching for snakes and critters. Max dropped and did his business then wagged his tail at me, looking all cute and proud of himself. He glanced behind me, and then his body stiffened. His growl rumbled low in his chest, and I whipped around and flicked on the light to where he was staring. Leila stood there waiting for us in the darkness. Max ran over and leaned against her, and she rolled him over on his back and rubbed his belly. His one leg began kicking at the air; apparently, she had found a tickle spot. She laughed at him and asked me if I had started the coffee yet.

I told her no, gave her a big hug, and went in to flick on the coffee pot and use the bathroom. I went back out to join her on the terrace when I was done with my morning business. She had pulled up a chair, and she was watching the water. The moon was reflected on the ripples, and the night was clear. It was getting light out but would be a while until the sun rose. She reached over and took my hand and smiled at me.

"I love rising early, well before the waking world ruins it with its endless noise and movement. It's almost sacred in its way, and until I began traveling, the idea of getting up at the butt crack of dawn was never appealing to me. But once I got out there and realized that there was so much to see, I didn't want to miss a thing. But morning, that's my new favorite time of the day, sitting with my thoughts, being grateful, and just inhaling the beauty of it all; that's life to me." She smiled, and I looked at her with admiration.

What a beautiful creature she is, I thought, with her head held high and this energy that oozed from somewhere within her. I was so proud of her, and I could see that my baby girl was growing into an amazing woman.

176

Max jumped down and was sniffing around the yard. I sat there absorbing the moment with Leila, knowing there was no place I'd rather be than sitting there in that moment of peace, and I felt my love for her overflow. I began crying. I was so happy. She asked me why I was crying. I found it so hard to explain just how much she meant to me.

I drank some coffee and listened as she talked more about her journey. I didn't have to go visit these places, because as she spoke, I was right there with her. Her descriptions were so vivid and detailed, and I looked at her and told her she needed to write it all down.

Not many people have the luxury to do what she had done, and she should share her words with others. She laughed and said that she had been journaling the experience, but that she'd think about it. I know she will do well with anything she does. She wanted to go back and finish the trail in Spain when Julia was able, and then she looked at me and smiled.

"I love her, Mom. I have to be honest with you. I've always been honest with you, and I can't hide my feelings. It kind of started before we left, but I didn't know the extent of it until we were traveling together. She is my other half, always has been, I guess. We are happy, and I love her. I love who she is. We are stronger together, and I hope you can come to understand it in time. I know the thing with Dad threw you for a loop, well, more than that, but I've always felt like I was different. I've known in a way, ever since I was young, and I don't think it's hereditary or anything. It is simply what it is."
I took a sip of my coffee and smiled at her, hugged her hard and looked into her bright blue eyes.

"I love it that we can talk like this, that you can tell me your thoughts and feelings. I've always loved that about us. I'm glad that you told me, but I already had figured it out. When you two are around each other, there's this undercurrent of attachment, this deep love that just sparks between you. I'm happy for you. I'm sad that I won't have any grandchildren, but I've got Max now, so I guess that counts a little bit. Your heart holds so much love, and I'm glad you found the right person to share it with. I like Julia, and I couldn't be prouder of the woman you've become. You'll always have my blessing Leila, always."

We sat together like that for a while, watching the waves and just being. I told her more about Raphael, and she was excited to meet him. I missed seeing him last night, being with him, but Leila and I needed time to reconnect, so I was glad for our time together.

Leila was going to bring Julia down to see the shop later in the morning, and I couldn't wait for her to see my newest creation. I told her about the cookies, and that made her happy to hear.

"You should have a bake section and sell them, maybe some cupcakes, too. You always made the best cupcakes. Remember the ones you made for me in fifth grade, how you hid those little prizes inside. I found the unicorn one, but you gave me enough hints, so I kind of knew which one to pick. I carried that with me in my bag when I left on the trip. The purple unicorn, he's my good luck totem. Although, maybe Julia was the one who needed him, what with the fall and all."

I told her I'd think about it, but I don't know if I want to be a full-time baker and gift shop owner. I'm enjoying baking the cookies a lot, though. We'll see, but you never know. Stranger things have happened.

Leila got up to go see if Julia was up, and I sat there watching Max romp in the yard. I'd have to figure out what I'd do with him once Leila left again. I couldn't leave him here all day alone but wondered if he'd enjoy sitting in the shop every day with me. He was a pretty mellow dog, so maybe he would. I could get him a doggy bed and train him to stay when someone came in. I could picture him decked out in a little doggy bandana, and I thought about the man with his dog in the stroller. I'm glad I have a rescue, even if he came by way of Spain. He stared at me, his little tail wagging back and forth, and he jumped up the stairs of the terrace one at a time, tentative and unsure, but he made it all the way up the five steps, and he seemed so proud of himself.

He wasn't one to jump all over you, either, and I was thankful for that, but he loved to be cuddled and carried around. I called him, and he followed me in to the kitchen and then he sat waiting patiently. I poured him some kibble out of the bag that Leila had left out on the counter. I wasn't sure how much to give him, so I filled the bowl half full. I turned to put it on the floor, and he was sitting up on his hind-quarters as if begging me. Damn, he's cute. I laughed and sat the food down and told him he was a good boy.

Leila came down, with Julia slowly making her way behind her. Leila had the crutches, and she waited until Julia made it to the bottom of the stairs, and she kissed her on the cheek as she handed her the crutches. Julia wished me a good morning, and I smiled at her. Leila told me that they trained Max to do the trick before he'd get his food. He was very smart and caught on quickly. He liked swimming too, she said, so I knew I'd have to take a trek down to Brohard Paw Park to do a swim at the beach and see how he did. She told me that he was sometimes timid around bigger dogs, but I was more concerned with other aggressive dogs behaving badly. There goes mother mode, already worrying about my newest charge.

I had to get ready for work, so I left the girls to their own devices. There were things in the fridge for breakfast, but I wasn't sure what their usual fare was. Leila said they were going to head downtown and hit the French bakery and she asked if she could borrow the Subaru. I told her it wouldn't be a problem. I still rode my bike to work and wouldn't need either vehicle. She was impressed that I rode daily, and she told me how good I looked. Work was agreeing with me, and I didn't mention the Raphael workout in bed factor. That was too much information, and I didn't want her to judge things until she met him. He was coming over for dinner tonight, and they'd finally meet. I wasn't nervous; I was excited.

I made it to work with time to spare and pulled out my flavor of choice for the day, ginger snap cookies with bits of candied ginger on top. I tried one just to make sure they made the transition from freezer to plate, and they were divine. I don't always eat one, but it's the first time I've made this recipe, and I wanted to make sure. I loved trying new recipes, and it kept going through my mind what Leila had said about expanding and doing baked goods for sale. My cookies were already a hit, but I would have to hire another person to cover me for kitchen time, and I'm still not sure about Max. I don't think they look kindly on cooking with an animal present. Things to ponder; it never ended, but it was a good thing. I was blessed.

The store stayed busy all day, sales were through the roof again, and Raphael was coming over for dinner, albeit a late one. The girls were out and about, and they took Max with them until I figured out what to do about that situation. I walked in the door to the silence of the house, and I realized I missed the little guy. I was making basic spaghetti and meatballs for dinner, and I had stopped and picked up a loaf of Italian bread that I was going to turn into cheesy garlic bread. I also stopped by Crate & Marrow and bought some toys for Max. I don't want my baby to be bored.

Raphael is in charge of the salad for dinner. He's a master at healthy eating and always puts together unique items in his salads, along with his homemade vinaigrette made with fresh squeezed juice; it makes my mouth water just thinking about it. A nice aspect of living in Florida is the freshest citrus that's available. I threw the meatballs in the microwave on defrost, realizing with dismay that they hadn't completely thawed out in the fridge. I checked the clock and saw that I had a few minutes to spare, so I went up to change my clothes.

The spaghetti request was Leila's choice. It had been months since she had it, and it was always her favorite growing up. When I made meatballs, I always tripled the recipe and froze the majority of them. Their flavor translated well from being turned into ice cubed meat, and with it being just Leila and me for what seemed like forever, we only needed a few at a time. I wasn't worried about the high carb aspect of the pasta, because with the store being so crazy busy, I was working off the calories every day and then some.

Leila and Julia walked in as I walked back into the kitchen, and my sweet Max came scrambling across the floor when he saw me; his tail was like a windshield wiper on high in a monsoon. I picked him up and he wriggled around, licking my face, and I swear he was smiling at me. Leila laughed and asked if she could help with anything, and I told her she could start the sauce. I had it ready to go; it just needed heating, and the meatballs would swim in it for a while. Raphael seemed to be running late, and I hoped he hadn't forgotten.

I set the table for four and listened as Leila told me about where they had gone. It sounded like they had an amazing day, and Julia did great managing the crowds on crutches without incident. The people down here are pretty friendly and helpful, one of the reasons I wanted to move here. I grabbed a bottle of red from the counter and the bottle of white from the refrigerator and opened them both. I poured three glasses, holding off on Raphael's until he got here. We walked out on the terrace and killed a few minutes, while we waited for him. I finally texted him, and he said he was on his way; he had to pick up a last-minute item. I wonder if he's nervous about meeting my baby girl.

I told Leila about my day, and she had loved the store. I didn't have much time to talk to them while they were in, but I had seen them moving through the rooms peeking at things. It's still just Bonnie and me, and when we get slammed with customers, it's hard to stop and chat. The register has been getting quite a workout, and I've been having to place more orders than is typical. It's a good thing, but at the end of the day, I'm physically drained. I've been thinking about hiring another part time girl or guy to help out, or else I'll be living there.

The sky looked like rain. Big clouds bubbled up on the horizon, and the air just hung heavy. You could see the lightning flashes, and we moved our little soirée indoors. We were puttering with the food when Raphael walked in, several bags in hand, and he dropped them on the counter and ran back out to his car. Leila looked at me with a big grin.

"Well, I must say Mom, not bad, not bad at all. He's a hottie." She looked at Julia, who laughed and nodded in agreement. Raphael came back in with what looked like a bakery box, and he handed it to me with a sparkling smile.

"Hey beautiful, this needs to be refrigerated." He walked over to Leila, his hand outstretched, and he introduced himself then repeated with Julia. Max looked at him warily and leaned against my leg. Raphael came and put his hand down for Max to sniff, and passing inspection, he petted him on the head gently and spoke to him in an easy tone.

"Cute dog, what's its name?" I told him that he was Max and that he'd be living here now. He didn't say anything about the new family member, but he gave me a kiss and started throwing the salad together after washing his hands. He told us how he had gotten tied up with an accident down at the marina and had to talk to the police, being the sole witness. He apologized but knew we could survive a few-minute delay. He sliced, diced, and chopped effortlessly, and he was done in five minutes flat. I timed him and then laughed when he was done. Super Salad man, all he needed was a cape to complete the scene.

He and I finished getting things ready, slicing the bread, draining the pasta, and throwing it all in a large porcelain bowl for serving. We sat down and enjoyed the meal while Leila peppered Raphael with questions, and he asked her and Julia both about their trip. I sat there pleased with the reception they gave him, and it felt nice to have an almost full family element to the evening. Nice conversations and good food, but Max clung to me all evening, and I wondered if it was the weather that made him skittish or Raphael.

The rain had moved in, and the thunder and lightning were in full-on storm mode beyond the windows; drops were hitting the roof with a vengeance. The lights flickered a few times when the heavy crash of lightning struck close by, and I hoped we didn't lose power. We had a generator, but I hadn't used it in ages. I should have had it checked, and I made a mental note to do that Sunday on my day off.

After dinner, Raphael cleared the dishes and brought out the box from the refrigerator and then went back to bring out four plates and forks. Inside the box was a decadent chocolate cake with coconut, pecans and chocolate bits. It looked heavenly, but I chose to have a small sliver, having had too many carbs with dinner, and I didn't want to go overboard.

Raphael and I washed the dishes while the girls drove down to the beach to watch the storm, and I think they wanted a little alone time, and that meant time for Raphael and me, too. Max sat moping beneath my chair, and I wondered if he was feeling well. He'd been kind of off since he and the girls got back. The kitchen was all tidy, and Raphael told me that he had an unexpected excursion chartered for three in the morning. They were going pretty far out on this trip, and he wanted an early start. The storm was supposed to be gone by midnight. He said he didn't want to interrupt my sleep, so he was leaving to catch some sleep of his own before he had to head out. I was disappointed and told him so. He kind of looked guilty, and then he smiled and kissed me softly and told me he'd make it up to me.

So, I now had the house to myself, and after he left, I went out onto the covered part of the terrace, a glass of wine in hand and Max at my heels. I picked him up and sat him in my lap, and even though it was hotter and muggier than Hades outside, I cuddled with him and gave him little kisses on his head. He wagged his tail and wanted down, set free. He ran down the steps and began zipping around the yard happily, chasing a lizard until it ran up a tree. The rain didn't seem to bother him in the least. Barking commenced as he darted from the lizard back to me, and he looked at me like I was supposed to help him get it down. Nope, sorry bud, not happening, I told him, and he gave me that little side-eyed look and wandered away, seeming to have forgotten about the lizard, at least for now.

I wondered what was up with Raphael. He knew tonight was important to me, and he engaged in the conversation but seemed distant somehow. I hope everything's okay with him, and even though he didn't seem overly enthusiastic about Max, it wasn't his dog, so oh well. But then again, Max wasn't gaga over him, either. Whatever, I certainly wasn't going to lose sleep over it. I sat there for a half-hour and then called Max and headed in. I grabbed a towel and dried him off. His hairs were sticking up all over the place, and he shook himself, sending any last residual water all over the tile floor.

My phone was blinking, and I had a message from Leila that she and Julia were going to head to Siesta Key to see if there was any nightlife happening there, and that they would be quiet when they came in. I assume she was giving us time alone together, but it was just going to be me and Max, so no love time for me, just puppy kisses.

I grabbed a book that I was a quarter of the way through and sat on the couch with my new best friend. I kicked my feet up on the ottoman and relaxed. The book was okay but not my usual fare, and I had a hard time getting back into it. I threw it down after ten minutes and flicked on the tv. I surfed the channels and found *The Andy Griffith Show* and settled in to watch that.

I never watched it as a kid, the show was a little before my time, but I caught a lot of the reruns. I had forgotten a lot of the episodes, so it was almost like catching it for the first time. They were on back to back, and it was nice. It was wholesome viewing and much better than the reality crap they're always spewing out. I have enough going on in my life. Why do I want to deal with someone else's drama? I guess I must have dozed off because I woke up when Max began growling. I figured the girls must be home, and I waited but nothing. I flicked off all the lights except for the one in the entryway, locked up, and headed up to bed.

Max snuggled up next to me, and I fell back to sleep within minutes, the carbs doing their duty and crashing me, along with the two glasses of wine I'd had. I heard the girls come in around two in the morning, and Max was on alert but must have known who it was, so he settled right back down. I'm not sure what kind of watchdog he'll turn out to be, but that's okay. That's what alarm systems are for, right?

Chapter Twenty

Repetitions of history, mermen...enough said.

I woke refreshed at five thirty in the morning and triggered the coffee pot to begin working its magic and hustled Max out the door to do his business. He was still waking up and stumbling around the yard, unenthusiastic about his duty, but he finally succeeded, and then he came back up to lean on me. I had to be at the shop at nine thirty and wasn't sure what time the girls would get up, having had the late night.

I remembered those days well, even though it was so many years ago. I can't say I was a wild child, because I wasn't, or at least not much anyway. I loved the idea of dancing but could only manage it with a few cocktails. The sad life of Destiny, I was born with two left feet and not much rhythm. I had swaying

187

down pat, though. I was a very good swayer. The coffee was ready, and I went and poured myself a huge mug, needing the extra jolt.

Leila joined me forty-five minutes later, and we watched the sky get lighter, enjoying the silence and just being at peace in the new day. She had a cup of coffee but wasn't touching it, and I teased her and asked if she was hungover. She'd never been a big drinker, but life happens and people can change. She told me she was designated driver last night, which, with Julia's leg, was understandable. She seemed to have something on her mind, but I've learned not to press, just let it flow on its own when she is ready.

"Did you and Raphael have fun last night?" She took a sip of her coffee, and I told her how Max and I had enjoyed a thrilling hour of *The Andy Griffith Show* and how Raphael had to leave due to the charter scheduled. She sat silently for a minute then looked me in the eyes. Her gaze held a serious edge to it that she often had when something was wrong.

"We saw him last night, Mom. He was at The Pink Flamingo Lounge, and he was with an older woman, I mean, like eighties, older. They seemed pretty chummy, too. We were in the back of the club, and he didn't see us, but they were out on the dance floor for the hour while we were there. How well do you know him? Are you two exclusive?" I sat there in shock, and she could tell the news came as a surprise to me.

"Why would he lie to me like that? I know he had been working in Siesta Key when we met, so he must know a bunch of people, but he told me he was going home. He had a charter scheduled to go out at 3 a.m., and he needed to go home and sleep." I was confused. We weren't having any issues, and he'd always been attentive. There's got to be some explanation for this, I thought, but I didn't know if I should just let it play out and see if he brings it up. Leila looked at me and sat silently as different scenarios played through my mind.

"You'll figure it out, Mom. You're strong, and I know you'll know how to handle it. You're a mermaid after all, and mermaids are beautiful and strong. They don't take any crap, but if you're really enamored with him, I would definitely suggest doing some kind of background check on him. He's smooth and pretty, but I could sense that something was off with him, and Max, well that dog has never met a person he didn't like, and he didn't seem too keen towards Raphael. I always trust a dog's judgement above all else."

"How friendly was he being with this woman last night? Friendly dancing, or kissing/dancing?" Her eyes told me what I needed to know.

"My friend Eileen works there, and I asked her in a roundabout way about him. She told me to steer clear, that the woman he was with was his widow-squeeze. Mrs. Bromely had lost her husband a few years ago, and Raphael has been her steady since. She's got tons of money and doesn't care if she spends it all before she dies. She's already given him a truck and a boat; next will be the house when she dies. He's a scammer, but Mrs. Bromely doesn't care. She's rich enough to do as she pleases, and he's her favorite boy-toy, has been for over two years now." She looked apologetic when she finished but knew she had to tell me, that I had the right to know who I was dating.

Raphael and I had never talked about being exclusive, but for the last few months, there had been many nights when he wasn't here, often for a fishing charter he had to lead, and I knew guys liked to fish super late at night, but up early for fishing isn't the same thing as dancing in a bar with some old cougar. I was going to look a little deeper, and I wasn't going to alert him that I knew anything. I'd just play it cool and wait until I had more information.

My last marriage was based on lies, and I wasn't about to give my heart to someone who was up to no good. Leila said she'd help me; she'd look up information on the computer, and I told her his birthdate and where he told me he was from, about his wife and son who perished, anything I could think of to funnel the information down, because I'm sure there are many Raphael Santos's in the world. She hugged me tight, and I was glad that she was there. I was going to need some emotional support through this, and who better than the true love of your existence? Leila had always been my world, and she was strong like me. Besides, had she not been here, I may have never known the truth about Raphael.

I had to go get ready for work, and I wanted a few minutes to be alone. I wanted to cry, and I needed to process, to meditate or something, and not allow this to ruin my day. Hope was going to be stopping by the shop, and I was excited to see her. She's been traveling all over India for the last two months, and I was excited to hear about her trip. Perhaps I'd make a date for lunch with her on Sunday and get her perspective on this whole scenario.

I felt like my heart was in pieces. I can't let a man break me. I refuse to let that happen. I've got to pull up my big girl pants and go through the process, and I knew it was going to hurt like a bitch, but I'm not going to be played like a fool, not by him, not by anyone. I jumped in the shower and let my tears flow freely, washing the sorrow down the drain at my feet.

I got to the shop a few minutes early and walked around straightening anything left askew from the last time I was in. Bonnie wouldn't be in for another hour, and I took the time to enjoy the quiet before turning on the music. I used a music service and contemplated what to flood the shop with. They didn't have a station for angry women, so I flip-flopped and finally decided on seventies tunes. Nothing like a little disco to take your mind off sucky, shit-heel men.

Raphael was supposed to text me when the "excursion" was over, and I knew now that could mean just about anything. Would it be the tryst with Mrs. B or another Mrs. whomever? Maybe he had more than one of us on his line. What a catch, my ass. Grrr…I'm so pissed. I wonder if he planned the whole thing, hooking me like a fish on the beach. Reel her in. She's a fighter, but she's looking for that big hook to pull her to shore. Quick, be the one to save her from herself. Get the net.

Had he done research on me? He seemed to like widows and just because a woman is on the beach single doesn't mean she's a widow. Now I was getting paranoid. I had to stop this. My thoughts were interrupted by a knock on the back door, and I looked around the corner to find Hope standing out on the step, smiling at me through the glass. I unlocked and opened it and threw myself into her arms as the tears started flowing full force. I was a wreck, and I was so happy to see her.

Hope held me away from her and touched my face. She wiped a few tears away, and I apologized. It seems I always feel like I'm needing to apologize for something. She followed me in, and we sat in the kitchen. The shop didn't open for another half an hour, and I told her about what Leila had seen up in Siesta Key. She nodded and listened. I was so grateful to have her in my life. The nice thing about Hope is she allows you to find your own answers. She doesn't try to sway your thinking one way or another, and as I spoke to her, I knew what it was that I'd have to do.

I could be spiteful and talk to Mrs. Bromley and ruin his chances, but that would be petty. I was a mermaid, and we don't do things like that. We cut our losses and learn and rise up to something better. There's always something waiting on the next horizon; you just have to have patience and be open to allowing the possibility of it. I could do it. I didn't need Raphael, and I didn't want to hear his excuses. It would be, "Sorry, but this isn't working for me. So, see you, buh-bye asshole." Okay, maybe I wouldn't use the word asshole, but I knew I'd be thinking it the entire time, and it just might slide out of my pie-hole. I told Hope what I was thinking, and she smiled and hugged me.

"You don't need me, love. You know what's right for you, and you're going to do it in style. You haven't lent him any money, have you?" I laughed loudly and shook my head.

"I liked him, but that would have raised my suspicions had he asked. He let on that he had more money than me anyway, what with his rentals in Puerto Rico. Damn, I wonder if any of his stories were true, come to think about it. Max didn't care for him much, either."

Hope looked at me strangely. "Who pray tell is Max? Do you have another gentleman friend already?" I grabbed my phone and pulled up his picture to show her my newest addition. She smiled and told me what a looker he was. I agreed and put my phone down, noticing the time.

"I've got to open shop, but do you want to go out to lunch this weekend, maybe Sunday? We can play catch up. If you want to do it sooner, I have Bonnie here now, and she can cover for me if we slip away for a little bit. I figured you'd want to get settled in."

Hope pulled out her calendar and said tomorrow would fine, and she'd drop by around noon. I told her that would be perfect, and I put it on my calendar so I wouldn't forget. She hugged me goodbye and went out the front as I unlocked it. There was one lady sitting out on a bench waiting, and I rushed back in to pull out today's cookie of the day, butterscotch chunk with sea salt and chocolate bits in a butter cookie. They were one of my favorites. I had made a monthly calendar with the cookie of the day listed, and after a while, I knew who to expect to see on any given day. My customers were loyal to a fault, and business was booming. I watched Hope drive away and felt blessed to have her in my life.

Leila and Julia stopped in around four o'clock on their way to the beach. They were heading to the dog beach with Max. I told her as they were leaving to "be careful and carry him until you get close to the water." She smiled and told me she knew and not to worry. But then, of course, I had to add, "Let him down on the wet sand and not the dry stuff, because it gets so hot down there that it will burn the little pads on his feet." She laughed at me and called me a mother hen. She held Max up to give me a quick lick goodbye, and then they shuffled off. I still had an hour left before closing time, and I checked my phone for any messages from Raphael.

Surprisingly, there was one that he had sent at two p.m. saying that he was leaving with another charter and that he'd have to take a raincheck for tonight. He said to enjoy my time with Leila, and he knew that, with company, I wouldn't miss him as much, but that he loved me and missed me. I wanted to send a scathing reply but just told him no problem. I'd see him when I'd see him, I thought to myself, and then you'll be gone baby, gone. Like a flash, Boom! Gone baby, yeah!

I still didn't know what to say to him, and I ran a million scenarios through my head all day but hadn't come to a definitive conclusion on what would be the best way.

Leila texted me a half hour after she left and said Max was loving the waves and not to make dinner; they were going to pick up a pizza on their way home. They'd be in around six or so. That worked out perfectly for me, not having to cook after a long day, and I wanted her and Julia's advice on how to handle the Raphael thing. I didn't have to worry about him stopping by, so we could have a girls' night kind of evening. I was happy and looking forward to relaxing and venting.

Bonnie left at four-thirty, and I was tidying up when a gentleman walked in. I had never seen him before, so I figured he must be a new snowbird. He said hello to me and walked around the shop looking at the art on the walls, then he picked up one of the local's books and tucked it under his arm.

"That's a really good book, and if you like suspense, then you're going to love her work. I've read it twice, and it never gets tiring. I get something new out of it every time I read it." I said to him as I straightened a shelf of glass sea creature figurines. I had a manatee in my hand, and I held it up to the light to look through it. I don't know, but comparing manatees to mermaids, I still have to wonder what the heck Columbus was thinking.

The man kept moving through the rooms, picking up items, and then he called me over as he stood in the children's section. He was holding one of the handmade mermaid dolls. They came with interchangeable bottoms, so that if the mermaid was going to a party, she could wear pink fins or purple or her basic teal. They all had sparkly bling on them, and a woman in town made them for me exclusively.

"Do these come with all the bottoms or do you purchase them separately?" he said, looking confused.

"They come with the basic teal greenish ones; the others you buy individually. They're easy to change from one to the other, but the one comes with the doll; the rest are fifteen dollars each." He handed me a blonde mermaid doll and grabbed a different fin outfit in each color that I had stocked.

"Do they make boy mermaids? Or is that just a girly kind of thing?" I chuckled and told them that legend has it that mermen do exist, but I only had girl mermaids, no boy ones yet.

"Are you buying this as a gift? Because I can gift wrap it, if it is." He shook his head no and said that he's just buying it because the grandkids were arriving that night, and he liked to

195

give them something to remind them of their vacation here. He asked if I had anything for boys, and I showed him some books on pirates and things like that. "Down on the Main Street, you'll find more items for boys, some shark teeth, sport things, and dinosaur books. I'm mostly sea related items here. Dinosaurs aren't my thing, but boys do like pirates, the last time I checked."

He grabbed a looking glass, pirate hat, and a book on pirates. I helped him carry it all up to the register. I offered him a cookie, and he took it, chewing on it with exuberance as I rang up his items.

"It's got to be exciting, seeing your grandkids again. How old are they?" I asked as he helped himself to another cookie.

"Mmm…these are spectacular," he said in between bites. "Do you sell these? I'd love to buy a dozen. I haven't had a cookie this good since I was a kid. My mom was an excellent baker, and her cookies were the best. I think yours might even be as good as hers. Sara is eight, and Liam is the oldest at ten. They're my daughter's kids, and she's kind of going through a messy divorce right now. She thought it would be good to have them get away and visit me for a bit, just until things cool down at home. It's been years since I've had small children around the house. My wife always handled that while I worked, but I was around for the teenage years when my wife got cancer. Sometimes they did their best to try your patience, but they grew up to be college educated and very good kids overall."

I took his credit card and bagged up the last eight cookies I had, smiled at him and told him no charge for the cookies, and that I hoped the kids enjoyed them as much as he did. He laughed.

"I hope they make it home so that the kids might get some, too. I'm Justin, Justin Hayward, and it's a pleasure to meet you. I'm finding that Venice is a town of transplants, and I'm from the finger lakes area in New York." I shook his hand and told him it was a pleasure to meet him, too. He told me that he had just moved to Venice a few months ago and hadn't had much of a chance to do any shopping in the local district, which explains why I had never set eyes on him all season. He had beautiful blue eyes and a charming smile. I could see how much he loved his kids when he talked about them, and I liked a man who spoke highly of family.

"I bet your wife must be thrilled to have some little ones running around again. My daughter is home currently from touring the world, and there's nothing I love more than falling asleep knowing my kid is safe under my roof again." I smiled at him as he looked at me, his eyes filled with a wistful look.

"Mari died a year ago. She gave it a good fight, but in the end, it won. I miss her every day, and this was our dream, to move down here. I decided I couldn't stay rattling around in that house up there without her, and I know she'd want me to keep on with our plans. I miss her, and we had picked out the house together, but when she got too sick, she wanted to be close to the kids so we stayed up north until she passed. She would have loved your cookies by the way. Her sweet tooth was unbelievable, and you thought mine was bad. Mari loved her sweets. Thank you, Destiny. It was a pleasure meeting you, and I know I'll definitely be back. How could I not, with such a nice store, good cookies and pleasant conversation?" He nodded to me once as I handed him his bag, and I watched him as he left.

Typical down here, another widowed customer. It seemed that we were a dime a dozen. I have no idea how old he was but guessed him to be in his early sixties. He seemed nice, and I knew he would be back because I had tucked a cookie schedule for the month in the bag with his items. I told you, if you can't get them in with tchotchkes, there's always the cookie factor.

It was quitting time, and I locked the door, did the till, and headed out. I didn't have to cook dinner, but I stopped at the Wine and Coffee store and picked up a few bottles for girls' night. I felt a lot calmer than I had that morning, and I told myself that I wasn't going to let the thing with Raphael ruin my night.

Chapter Twenty One

Oh yes, it's ladies' night and hell hath no fury.

Leila and Julia were in the pool when I got home. Two boxes of pizza were on the kitchen counter, and Leila was floating around on this huge swan with Max on her lap. She was wearing her sunglasses and a big floppy hat, and I pulled out my phone to capture the moment. Max looked so cute. He wagged his tail when he saw me come out, and Leila broke out her best selfie smile when she saw that I was taking a picture. Julia was on a big yellow rubber duck off to the side. Her hand was holding on to the bar to the stairs, and her casted leg was propped on the edge of the concrete, keeping it safely out of the water. She had her leg wrapped in a white kitchen trash bag for extra protection, and I hoped they were the waterproof kind, just in case. I changed angles and moved over so that I could get all three of them into one shot.

I love casual moments like this, when everyone is relaxed and having fun and there's just this really good feeling to it. I asked them if they wanted some wine, and they both said yes, so I went in and poured us some big plastic cups of Pinot Grigio. I have these great Tervis wine glasses that won't break or sweat. I find that, once the wine starts flowing, accidents tend to happen, and I hate the idea of any broken glass near the pool.

Leila came over on her floaty to get her glass, and Max jumped off, ran over to me, and began sniffing my legs, as if I'd been to the Crate & Marrow getting him treats. He's a smart little guy, and I pulled a snack out of my pocket for him after he sat and begged. He hasn't had any accidents in the house, and I'm thankful that he got over that period of his life while off with Julia and Leila. The best kind of dog, one who's so cute and already trained.

I didn't feel like swimming. I prefer going in after sundown when the world quiets down and the air gets a little cooler. I watched a boat off in the distance and felt my mind wandering to thoughts of Raphael.

"Penny for your thoughts? Mom, what's going on in that beautiful head of yours? How was your day at work? Did you make your million yet?" She said smiling, and I think I knew what she really wanted to ask, but she held off.

I noticed she didn't ask me about Raphael in her barrage of questions, and I knew she was waiting for me to bring up the subject. I told her about Hope stopping by and about the last man who had stopped in, Justin. Other than that, as far as I was concerned, it was just a typical day on the island.

She floated around on the swan and kicked her legs in the water. I remembered being that age, young and carefree. I enjoyed my age now. I never wanted to be one of those women who were angry all the time over aging. There's not a damn thing we can do about it, so why not enjoy it? Raise hell in better ways, I say.

"Where on earth did you get those pool floats? They're adorable. I've looked at them before in the stores, but I never got around to buying one. " She kicked her feet until she was closer to the edge and handed me her now empty glass.

"Down in South Venice, one of those pools stores had them on special, and I figured this way Julia could kind of swim, or at least be in the pool without getting her cast wet. So, I bought one for her and one for me. You inherit them when we leave, so you'll have your choice." I smiled at her and pictured Raphael and me floating around while lazing in the sun.

"Damnit, I've got to stop this." I must have said it out loud, because Leila looked at me with her eyebrows raised.

"Did I do something wrong?" she said, looking confused and concerned.

"No love, I was just picturing Raphael and me. I've got to stop doing that. It's obviously not going to work. I won't let it work, certainly not now, knowing what I know. I just have to talk to him and tell him to piss off the next time he calls." Leila shook her head at me sadly.

"I know how hard this must be for you. It seems like you really liked him, Mom, but it gets worse. You might want to sit down. I did a little more digging around this afternoon. He's not from Puerto Rico. He grew up in Miami, and he's an ex-con. He was arrested several times in his youth. They have some of the records sealed, but he served time in prison for fraud. Apparently, he drained an elderly woman's bank account, all while he was supposedly her caretaker. She's passed away since, but her kids went after him when her fortune dwindled. They could only prove some of his theft, because she signed off on the other withdrawals and didn't have any mental issues at the time. I think he played her like he's playing you. He was never married either, and no child, so to tug at your heartstrings like that with his sob story of losing them off a cliff, well, he's just an asshole as far as I'm concerned. Thank God you didn't give him any money. You didn't, right? I meant to ask you that before."

I listened to her words and felt hollow. I wondered if I could ever trust anyone again. I couldn't believe how he had played me, and then I got really pissed off. For him to lie about something as tragic as losing a family, oh my God, what a scumbag.

I asked Leila what she thought I should do, and she said she'd think about it and come up with something good. Blowing him off without telling him why would serve no purpose. I was fed up and angry, and he was going to have some answering to do.

I looked at Leila and asked her how she found out about his police record.

"I have a friend on the force who helped me, but I can't say who, because I don't want him to lose his job over it. I only needed the information on his past, not any current address or anything like that, so he looked him up. I also found out that every Wednesday night, he and his old lady go to The Flamingo to dance. Didn't you notice his absence every Wednesday?"

I thought back, and I couldn't be sure, but I could see the truth in it. I'd been so busy with the store opening, and he wasn't over every night, just a few times a week. Maybe he told her he had a fishing excursion just like he had told me. I wouldn't doubt it. It was Friday, so I'd have some time if I wanted to confront him then. I would just have to make excuses in the meantime. I told Leila that I wanted to plan something around that, walking in and doing a face to face with him and his sugar mama. She said she'd think of something even better, and I knew that she'd come up with a doozy. Whatever it was going to be, I just didn't want to get arrested doing it.

The girls got out of the pool and went to get changed, and I slipped out of my work clothes and into a sundress. It was balmy out, and I brought the pizza out to the covered area on the terrace so that we could have some shade while we ate. The pizza smelled wonderful, and it was thin crust, a definite plus. I really had to start watching my carbs again. I cleared my mind of all thoughts related to Raphael and just decided to enjoy my evening with the girls.

The girls came down a half-hour later, all showered up and fresh in matching caftans. The embroidery work was so elegant, their garments were incredible, and they told me about the huge bazaar where they had found them while in Spain. They were pricy, but they only made that one splurge, Leila made a point of saying. Julia told me more about their travels while Leila snacked on a slice, and I noticed they'd constantly finish each other's sentences. They were good together, and I could tell they had a healthy relationship built on common ideas and respect for one another. I was happy for them both and told them so. I accepted their togetherness and couldn't have been any happier for them both.

My phone pinged, and I glanced at it quickly. It was Raphael texting me. I read his words, asking how my day was, and I sneered at the screen. I flipped my phone over on the table, switched it to off, and chose not to respond. I'd have to deal with it sooner or later but not right now. I refuse to let him intrude on my family moment of peace and simplicity.

We drank a little more wine, talking about the girls' future traveling plans, and we watched the sun die off on the horizon, content in each other's company. I was glad they were here, and Max too, although he was crashed out on a rumpled-up towel spread on the lounger, his little legs kicking in a puppy dream.

As it got darker, the mosquitos started buzzing me. I must be sweet or something because they always dive-bomb me like I am a free and easy blood bank. We decided to escape into the house and watch a movie and save my blood for my own use. I really just wanted to curl up and read a book, but I got the sense that the girls were enjoying my company and wanted me to hang out for a while with them. I offered to make some popcorn, but no one was really hungry for any, so we plunked down on the couch and checked out Prime to see if there was anything worthy on.

Roadhouse was an option offered by Julia with a smile, but Leila wanted *The Breakfast Club*. It didn't matter to me what we watched, so we flipped a coin and Leila won. I hadn't seen that movie in years but found myself engaged in it all over again. Ah, those teen years, I love a good romance, but the teenage angst, I don't miss it; that's for sure.

Once the movie ended, I bade the girls goodnight and headed up to the bedroom. I wasn't sleepy but needed some time to unwind and ponder my next move with Raphael. Max followed me up, yawning the whole way as he hopped up each step, and I was happy. Our time together was always filled with cuddles and kisses, and he was bonding to me as if he knew that he was staying behind when the girls left. Julia's cast wouldn't come off for another two months, so I knew I'd have the girls around, which might make the Raphael factor that much easier to contend with. I wouldn't be coming home to an empty house each night after work, and the conversations were always plentiful.

The girls were great. They did their thing but pulled their own weight around the house. I didn't feel like I had to tend to all their needs, and basically, my life just moved forward at its usual pace. They often cooked dinner, too, which saved me having to take on that chore. Many days, I would just have a salad or something, too tired after a long day to put together much else. They also liked organic and healthy fare for the most part, another plus in my dieting. I was keeping my weight off, and with the work load, lifting boxes and all the maintenance on the shop, I was getting toned up as well.

I lay in bed and thought about Raphael. I lived without him before, and I intended on doing it again. There were other fish in the sea. I just felt like such a fool. I wracked my brain looking for any signs of his deceit and found no red flags. It didn't matter though. He was out of here as far as I was concerned. I didn't need someone like that in my life, and I made a note to not beat myself up over something that I had no part of. He was the jerk, not me. He was the asshole, liar, con artist, and I wasn't. Let him hurt someone else; he was done hurting me. But now, I just needed to get over the loss of a friend aspect. I had confided in him, and he had betrayed me. That, to me, was unforgivable.

I meditated to a podcast, my earbuds planted firmly in my head as I petted Max. I was determined to fall asleep in a peaceful place, confident in my need to be a bigger person and to let him go gracefully and with my head held high. I owed that to myself.

I was a warrior mermaid, and no man could ever take that away. I needed to be claiming my strength, not allowing myself to be a victim. I promised myself that tomorrow was another day to be a new and stronger me, and I knew I was capable of it and more. I fell asleep at peace with letting him go and of allowing in something new and better, and I felt calm and content.

Chapter Twenty Two

Breaking up is so easy to do... when you're a mermaid.

In the morning, I decided I was going to take Max to work with me. I had everything set up and ready to go: food, a water dish, toys, and a cute little doggie bed for him to crash out on if he chose to do so. I figured, if he was going to be a regular fixture there, there was no time like the present to start training him to his new job as assistant doggy manager. He seemed like the kind of dog who was content just to be near you, and I knew he would fit right in.

I had told Bonnie about Max joining us, and I'm not sure if she likes dogs, but she didn't jump up and down in joy about it, nor did she pooh-pooh the idea either. I hate the idea of leaving him home all day, especially if I get held up late. He should be able to do his business more regularly than every nine hours.

The girls got me one of those kits that test your dog's DNA as a thank you gift, and we sent in a few pieces of hair. I was guessing he was some form of Scottish or West Highland terrier mix. In a few weeks, we will find out what our little Max is. As long as they don't try to tell me he's a Great Pyrenees or something stupid like that, it will have been worth whatever they paid.

I got to work, pulled out the cookie of the day, a shortbread with cranberries and orange zest, let Max sniff around to get the lay of the land, and he found his area within a few seconds. He curled up in his bed and watched me as I set up the store to open. Bonnie wouldn't be in for another hour, and the day looked like it was going to be another scorcher. Business can go either way on days like that. Some folks will go down to the beach to cool off, and others will go shopping to utilize someone else's A/C to cool off. I'm finding, with the elderly, they like it a balmy eighty degrees or more in their homes. With my hot flashes, I think I'd die if I had to deal with that. Bonnie seemed comfortable with ours here at 75 degrees, and she laughs at me when I stand below the vent holding my shirt open to let the cool air flow through to chill out the girls.

Menopause symptoms were pretty low, and my moods weren't off the wall. I had my own business that I could be proud of, and I was now single again. I felt as if I had the world at my fingertips. I hadn't heard from Raphael, and I didn't text him either. If he was worried, he certainly wasn't beating down the door to find out what was up. I was glad for the respite. I had just opened the door, and Maeve was sitting out on the bench fanning herself as she waited impatiently.

"It's about time, good God. Couldn't you open any sooner? I saw you moving around in there, so I know you were here. I checked my cookie schedule, and I see my favorites are on for today's flavor. Please tell me you didn't change it up on me." She hefted her bulk up off the bench and huffed and puffed her way into the store.

I shook my head at her and refused to let her ruin my day. I liked Maeve well enough; it's just that she's one of those people who will use you for what she can get. She'll stand there and eat cookie after cookie, and then try to grab a few to put in her purse for later. Once she cleaned off the whole plate between her pie-hole and her purse before I caught wind of what she was up to. I had only put four cookies out today, knowing they would be her favorite to clean me out of.

"No Maeve, your favorite is the flavor of the day, but I fell behind and wasn't able to make very many, so if you could just take one and leave some for everyone else, I would really appreciate it." She raised her eyebrows at me and harrumphed like I was causing her some severe hardship.

"Well, if you can't make enough for everyone, why do you bother then?" I held my tongue and placed one cookie on a napkin and handed it to her, subtly pushing the rest of the plate back out of her reach.

"Well, Maeve, I do it because I love to bake, and I give them away for free because most people are nice enough to not overindulge and spoil it for the rest. I'd hate to have to stop, and if I can only make so many, well, that's just my prerogative. I feel no need to explain."

She ate her cookie and looked around the shop with her shrewd and critical eyes.

"I see you haven't gotten anything new. Is business okay? You're not planning on shutting down or anything, right? Why don't you ever run a sale? I see all sorts of new things in other shops, and your prices are pretty steep compared to the rest, you know. Well, I have to go do some shopping. Thank you for the one little cookie," she said as she eyed the plate. She looked as if she was contemplating if I'd move away so that she could get another. I held firm and stood there as the wheels turned in that little hamster mind of hers, and she finally turned and left.

She never bought anything from the store, and as far as I could see, she only came in to eat all my cookies and speak ill of my shop. I can do without people like her, but my patience only extends so far. I wasn't going to let her rattle me, and once I saw her turn the corner, I heaped that plate sky high with dozens of cookies. I laughed to myself for being smart enough to outwit her. Score one for Destiny and zip for Maeve.

The bell rang, and I turned to see Justin walking through the door with his two grandkids in tow. He smiled when he saw me, and Max took a cue to get up, stretch out, and go see the kids. I guess he had a thing for kids, and they seemed excited, holding their hand out for him to sniff it instead of jumping all over him. He wagged his tail, apparently giving the okay that he was cool with them, and they wandered around the shop with Max following closely behind.

Justin came over and looked at the cookies on the plate. He looked at me as if to ask permission first, and I gestured for him to help himself. He took one and held it, inhaled the scent of the orange, and grinned from ear to ear. He took a bite, and I knew that I had scored again with this recipe. It was a favorite of most who took one, so I always made extra.

"These are amazing, Destiny. I'm going to have to buy at least a dozen of them to go." I laughed out loud and told him I really only made them for the customers to snack on while they shopped. I wasn't mass producing them. He nodded and called to the kids, who were engrossed in the children's section. They came out sporting huge smiles as they noticed the cookie platter. Sara held another mermaid in her hand. This one was an African-American mermaid with her colorful hair in braids running down her back.

"Can I get another one, Poppy? Bella may get lonely, but if I get her a friend, she'll be happy." Justin looked at me and rolled his eyes.

"Bella is the name of the mermaid I bought her. I guess she needs a friend. Who knew mermaids could be lonely? I thought they rode dolphins and whales all day and sang songs." I looked at him and smiled.

"Oh, mermaids can be lonely. They like to be around their sea creatures, but it doesn't take the place of someone to talk to." Sara stood there nodding as if to back me up, and I smiled at her.

"You must be Sara. Your Poppy told me you and Liam were coming to visit. I take it that you liked Bella, huh?" Sara held out her hand and introduced herself.

"We're not supposed to talk to strangers, but if I know you, Poppy says it's all right. What's your name?" I told her I was Destiny, and she told me that it was a very pretty name.

"If Poppy buys me another mermaid, I can name her Destiny. That's a very nice mermaid name I think. Destiny and Bella, best friends forever."

I looked at Justin, and he nodded yes to the mermaid and picked up another cookie. He asked the children if they wanted one, and they each said yes, please, and he handed them each one on a napkin.

"Make sure you don't spill crumbs on the floor. Miss Destiny here doesn't want to have to clean up after kids." Max walked over and sat down at Justin's feet and stared up at him with those puppy dog eyes that he makes when he wants something.

"I'm not buying you a mermaid, little dog, and I don't think your mommy would appreciate me giving you a cookie, either." He reached down and let Max sniff his hand, and Max sat back up in his begging position. Justin burst out laughing and looked at me.

"He sure knows how to tug on the old heart strings, doesn't he? Do you have any dog treats? I don't want to give him people food; it's never good to give a dog people food."

I was impressed that he knew proper dog etiquette, and I walked back into the kitchen to get Max a biscuit. I handed it to Justin, and Max held his position, begging for his snack. He handed it to Max, who took it over to his dog bed and began crunching loudly.

"Cute little dog, what breed is he?" I told him I wasn't sure what breed he was, but I told him how I came to be Max's new owner, and he smiled and shook his head.

"I haven't had a dog in a few years. After the last one broke my heart, and then with Mari getting sick, a dog just wasn't on my itinerary, but I'm certainly not adverse at getting one. Maybe now that I'm down here and settled. He's a perfect size. Will he be getting any bigger?"

I glanced over at Max, who finished his biscuit and must have known that he was the subject of conversation. His eyes moved back and forth between Justin and me, as if he were watching a tennis match.

"I think he's going to stay that size, and yes, it's perfect. I don't have to worry about him dragging me around on a leash. He's actually a pretty mellow dog, too. He's a cuddle bug at night, and best of all, he makes me smile. Nothing better than waking up to a sweet pup licking you on your nose when it's time to rise and shine."

Justin turned as Liam asked if they could go to a shop that carried boy stuff, and then he looked at me apologetically.

"It's okay, Liam. I know I don't have a lot of things here for boys, but I'll look into it for the future, okay?" He smiled at me and nodded politely. His daughter had done a good job. Both kids seemed very pleasant and well-mannered, and not a single cell phone was in sight.

213

I bagged up Destiny the mermaid while Justin pulled out his credit card, and then I wrapped up a dozen cookies for him to take home.

"How much for the cookies?" he asked, and I told him not to worry about it. He shook his head no.

"I insist. You've got to make a living just like everyone else, and if I'm going to keep dropping in to buy cookies, I insist on paying you for them." He handed me a ten and waved off any change.

"Buy some more supplies. I see some good ones coming up on the schedule, and it's on my fridge so that I can see it every morning. You'll be seeing me regularly, and I will consider you my go-to source for cookie replenishment, deal?" I smiled at him and tucked the ten in the till.

"I will do just that, and thank you, Justin. It's always a pleasure." He rallied the kids up and turned to leave. The kids shuffled out the door ahead of him, and Justin held it open as Raphael walked in. I must have had a look on my face as I saw him because Justin hesitated for a moment as Raphael stalked up to the counter. I nodded to him that it'd be okay, and Justin turned to leave. He looked torn though, and it made me feel good.

"What's going on with you, Destiny? I've left messages, I've texted, and I thought for a minute you were sick or something when you didn't get back to me." He began to walk around the counter, his arms outstretch to hug me, and I held my hand up.

214

"How was your fishing trip Wednesday?" I asked nonchalantly, and then I put space between us by pulling out some tissue paper from below the counter. I started folding them in half, readying them for future purchases, and he gave me an odd look.

"It went great, and they extended it into a two-day trip. That's why I haven't called. There is no reception out there. You're not mad, are you? I made a boatload of money on that trip, and I knew you didn't need my help here, what with Bonnie here most days now. I'm sorry if you needed me and I wasn't here. Honestly, it won't happen again." He walked around the shop and then spotted Max. He got low to the ground and called him to come, but Max wasn't budging.

"Good dog, extra treats for you tonight," I thought to myself and smiled.

"I'm not mad, Raphael. It's just that, with the girls here, I've been kind of busy. Honestly, it won't happen again..." A group of three women sauntered through the door in their big floppy hats and sunglasses. Hope was in the lead.

"I really can't talk right now, maybe tomorrow. I have plans with the girls tonight." I looked at him without skipping a beat. My voice was strong, and even though inside I felt like screaming at him, I think I handled it pretty damn well. I didn't want to make a scene, and he wasn't worth my breath, as far as I was concerned.

Hope smiled brightly and came around to hug me and glanced at Raphael.

215

"Do I know you?" she said to him, and he shook his head no, then told me that he'd talk to me tomorrow and left.

Hope looked like she was thinking of something, and she said, "I know where I know him from. That's Mrs. Bromley's boy toy, 'Raphi,' or something like that. That boy's a charmer, that one is. He tried to pick me up once down at The Crows' Nest when she went to the bathroom. Can you believe that?"

She introduced her two friends to me, old college chums who were in town visiting unexpectedly. Ellie and Kitty were twins. They were down for a week and staying with Hope.

"I brought them shopping so that they can spend some of their husbands' loot. I told them this was the best place in the world to spend it, and that I was friends with the owner. I also told them that you make the best cookies on this planet. What have we got good today?"

I felt sick to my stomach. Hope's words about Raphael reopened the already festering wound, and I knew that I had to get him out of my head and make it through the rest of the day.

"Cranberry orange zest shortbread, would you like one?" I said with a small smile, and they all picked one off the tray, munching and muttering about how good they were.

Ellie and Kitty wandered off to shop, and Hope could tell that something was wrong. I told her in a nutshell about Raphael and me, how Leila had found out more dirt on him. I wanted to cry, and she came around and hugged me tightly, telling me that it would be okay, and that I was much better off knowing before we had gotten too deeply involved.

"You didn't give him any money or co-sign a loan or anything, did you?" she asked, and I laughed and shook my head no.

"Everyone keeps asking me that. No, and he doesn't even have a key to my house, thank God. I only give keys to those who live there; that's an old rule I have, though he did ask me for one once. I told him it went against my principles and left it at that. I just don't know how to tell him to piss off without explaining why. I want to be a good person, and I want to kill him at the same time. I'll think of something, but in the meantime, if he keeps sniffing around, I'm just going to have to explain it. He's the liar, and I don't feel like I should even have to talk to him. Let him wonder, that's if he even cares." Hope shook her head back and forth and smiled.

"You wouldn't have to explain anything. The next time you see him, just ask him how Mrs. Bromley is doing. I would think he would know then loud and clear that you've got his number, and he'll be the one walking away. No muss, no fuss, just 'How's Mrs. Bromely?' He's been with her for years now, and last I saw, it looked like they were still hot and heavy. She is his meal ticket, and if he thought he was going to trade her in for you, he hasn't done it yet, and he knows he'd be a fool to throw away all his hard work. Besides, you deserve better, my little mermaid, and so much more, so just be done with him and get that weight off your shoulders. You'll feel better for it. Trust me."

I knew I was going to be pondering her comments for the rest of the day, and I saw a lot of sense in it. I didn't have to listen to his excuses. I didn't have to find the courage that I knew was swimming below patiently waiting to surface. I could just cut him off like a cancer and live my life.

Bonnie came in as the ladies were leaving, and I told her I needed to take Max for a walk. She looked at him with trepidation, and I told her how to approach him. She put her hand down where he could sniff it, but she was visibly shaking. I asked her if everything was okay, and she told me she had been bitten as a child and was worried he'd do the same. Max sensed her hesitation and came up to her slowly and sniffed her hand, then he sat up in his adorable begging stance. She smiled when she saw that he wasn't trying to jump all over her or act aggressively, and she patted his head twice and then stood up.

"I think that's enough for now. It's going to take me a little while, but as long as you know for sure that he won't bite me, I can learn to live with him being here." I handed Max a biscuit, knowing Bonnie wouldn't be ready to get that close to his choppers, and he ate it then cleaned up any crumbs he left on the floor. I grabbed his leash and took him out the back door. There was a little park down the street, and I had a whole roll of poop bags ready to go but knew I'd be surprised if I used even one.

The squirrels were out in force, and Max tugged after them only once. I corrected him, and he looked at me with those wise little eyes, and then he stopped, staring at something behind me, his body on alert, tense.

I turned and saw Raphael coming my way at a brisk pace. I moved beneath an oak tree to shade Max and me, seeing no sense in having the poor dog standing on the hot sidewalk. Raphael had a big smile on his face.

"I was going to stop back in and see if you wanted to go out to lunch, but here you are. I saw that Bonnie was at the shop, and she can cover things while you escape for a while. Maybe we can eat outdoors where Max can join us, unless you want to drop him off first, then we can go somewhere and eat inside where it's more comfortable. It is pretty hot out here today, huh?"

I took a deep breath and just gazed at him. All trace of good feelings had dissipated like a wild wind after a storm. There were so many words that I wanted to say, so much venom rising up in me towards him, and then it felt like a cool breeze washed over me, and I thought about Hope's words of wisdom. I took another breath and smiled at him sweetly.

"How is dear Mrs. Bromely, by the way?" I said and waited. I was watching as a thousand thoughts ran across his face. He stammered for a minute, and I could tell that he was trying to formulate some sort of reply that would appease me. I looked at Max and smiled.

"Come on, Max. I think we're done here." I walked away and left him standing there. He didn't say anything, probably because, what could he say? I walked towards the park, and neither Max nor I looked back. I felt free, and I silently thanked Hope for her ever-wise words. They were few, but just enough that I didn't have to feel bad about saying something that I would later regret. I was free, and I was moving forward. This mermaid warrior had won her battle without losing anything that really mattered.

Chapter Twenty Three

Yet again, more hellos and goodbyes.

Hey Kate,

I know it's been quite a while now, and I often wonder why I still bother. You're what glues me together on the toughest of days, and I appreciate your help in expanding my thinking and for allowing me to document my stories. Learning about myself over the past few years has had its good and bad points. I'm stronger now for it and thankful for every day that I can wake up in this paradise and know the feeling of immense gratitude as it flows through me. I know it all started with wanting to be a mermaid, and I still believe there is no issue in continuing to believe in my dream.

I have become my own best friend, and I have my best interest at heart. I am a mermaid, and my shrink has said that she doesn't see any need in me having to continue with her. She realizes I'm not going to go off the deep end, and I believe she was a help, so don't get me wrong, but I agree that I've gone as far as I need to for now.

Life is a good teacher, and as I've found, there are many people that will come in and out of your life. I find the difference is in not putting all my stock into someone or something other than what I know will be best for me. I always thought that it was a selfish way of thinking, but I know it's just me being true to myself. I live honestly, and I cannot lie, even to myself.

I spent a good chunk of my life with Alec, watching as he lived his life based on an ultimate lie, then learned another hard lesson with Raphael. I truly believe that what I want and what matters to me is what will be most important to my sanity. It's a form of self-preservation. I don't close myself off from others, but if they need too much or cling, I can't be that person to them. There's nothing worse than being suffocated and drowned while you try to save another soul that only wants to pull you down into the darkness with them.

I think that's what I see as a mermaid state of mind, to be free to swim away, to dream beneath a star filled sky, and to live in simple elegance surrounded by blue green seas and cloud-filled skies. I think I gravitated to Raphael because I was lonely, and he did teach me an important lesson. But I am strong alone, too. The choice will always be mine, and that brings me comfort.

I haven't heard from him since that day on the sidewalk, and I did thank Hope the next time I saw her for her timely advice. Business is thriving, and I've expanded into full-time baking. The store has been re-branded as Destiny's Dreams and Delights. Business has tripled since I began offering select catering of cakes and baked goods, and I hired another helper so that Bonnie doesn't have to live at the shop full time. My time is very balanced, and I am free to do what I do best, create with love and sugar. Max is doing great, not being a pest to the customers, and he enjoys just hanging around being close to me, my sweet shadow. Not a single soul has said a word about baking in the shop with Max there, and I hope it stays that way.

Leila and Julia headed back to Spain last week to finish their hike. Julia's leg is as good as new, and I was sad to see them leave, but I've got enough on my plate to keep me busy. I told Leila finally about Liam before they headed out. I know full well that keeping secrets would be my undoing. He was gone, and back then, I had my reasons, but I didn't want to go to my grave keeping something like that locked away.

I let it be free, setting the load down and allowing myself to live unburdened. I think she understood my reasoning; at least, she said she did. She is a strong one, and I think I cried more than she did when I told her. I pointed out the rippling waves that were rolling in and out before us and told her that he was always there for me. He would be there for her too, if she wanted to join in cherishing his being.

In our youth, we make tough choices. They may be right or wrong, but we live with the consequences for the rest of our days. I've carried the burden for twenty-plus years now, and it was freeing to be able to speak of him without guilt.

I cried when I said goodbye to them both, and Leila is going to try to keep in touch more frequently than she had before. I think, with me being so accepting of their relationship and of finally telling her about her twin brother, it's forged a closer bond between all of us.

I kept studying the yoga video until I felt I was competent enough to join the beach class. I make it a point to attend every Saturday morning at dawn because I found that my body feels so much better when I'm done. I come away feeling balanced and filled with peace, two things a mermaid thrives on.

I did get quite the surprise a few weeks ago, though. Justin was there for the class, and I smiled as I saw him arrive with his bright blue yoga mat. I haven't spoken much about him, and there's not a whole lot to say, but I enjoy his company when he stops by the shop. He talks about his wife often, and I can tell that he's still grieving. I listen and offer support, knowing how hard losing your soulmate can be. I make him some special cookies a few times a week, and I know he isn't eating them all, or else he'd be bigger than he is. Maybe it's the yoga keeping the pounds at bay, but he didn't look as if he fully comprehended all the moves, so I know he isn't doing it at home and on his own. I know how it feels being the newbie in class, because he looks like he's where I was when I first began. I told him I'd be happy to lend him my videos so he can study. It's a great workout, and peace and serenity are an amazing gift to walk away with when you're done.

I've got to go now, and not sure when I'll get time to write. I'm having some very busy days, and there's never much time to spare. I guess I just wanted you to know that I'm doing fantastic, that life is amazing, and that I don't depend on writing my feelings out quite as much as I used to. Thank you for listening though, and maybe I'll be back. We'll see, okay?

All right, so I'm back...I got to the shop earlier than normal, and it seems now with Max in my universe, I'm waking up bright and early every day. I had a rush phone order due today for a special cake for some kind of celebration. It was paid in full, and I am hand-delivering it after work today. I wasn't told if it was for something specific, just directions to make a beautiful red velvet cake with buttercream frosting and live floral decorations on top. It had to be enough to feed six, which to me is pretty easy to do, with not many layers to make. I got right to work on the cake after flicking on the radio.

They're calling for a tropical storm to blow through, and I want to get this done early, just in case the power goes out. The power can be touchy at times on this block, and I haven't failed yet in delivering on an order, and I don't wish to start now. It's my birthday today, but I don't have any plans. I'm thinking that I'm going to treat myself to pizza after I drop off this cake. It's been a long time since I've had pizza, and I deserve a treat.

Things are going okay. I've got to get to my doctor to get checked out, because I'm getting more forgetful. I left the stove on at home the other day; that's something I never do. I had Max with me at work, and it kind of freaked me out when we got home and I saw that the light on the stove was on. I've been forgetting other things, too. I ordered something twice because I couldn't remember ordering it the first time. The company was kind enough to take one of the orders back, but I had to pay a restocking fee. Then, I forgot to add the sugar to a batch of cookies I was making for the shop.

Bonnie told me that I seemed distracted a lot these days, so that excused it, but I know myself and I know I was not thinking of anything in particular while I baked. I wasn't woolgathering; I was just doing what I had always done. I've made those cookies a hundred times, and I keep knocking myself for it. I've got to breathe and let it go. It just bothers me, and I am deciding to be proactive about the whole thing. My memory has never been the greatest, but with the girls gone, I don't have anyone to keep an eye on me. If I can't trust that my head's functioning correctly, then I need to find out why and fix it.

I told Hope, and she was adamant that I go in and get looked at. I have an appointment for some blood work tomorrow, and I'm worried, but I guess I am coping as well as I can.
The cake looks beautiful. I put the finishing touches on it with some live pansies. It's one of the most elegant cakes I've ever created, and I took a picture of it to add it to my website.

I took Max to the park down the street again, and we sat at a bench and people watched for an hour. I know the shop is good to go with the girls in charge, and I don't have to leave to deliver the cake until later. I let Max off his leash to chase a squirrel, but he's good about coming right back when I call him. We left to head back to the shop, and I got confused for a minute. I take this route several times a week, and for just a few seconds, I lost my bearings. I ended up going down the wrong street but managed to walk around the block to get back to where I needed to be. I started crying because this is scaring me. I feel good. I get tired more often, but to get lost walking down the street. There's something wrong, and now I'm fearing what I'll find out with the testing.

At the end of the day, I grabbed Max and packed up the cake for delivery. I put the address into the phone and headed towards the customer's home. It was off the island and traffic was brisk; everyone must have been heading home for the day. I listened to the voice on the GPS as it told me to turn, when to turn and at one point. I couldn't get in the lane I needed to be in, and I had to go down and turn around to hit the light. The sun was blazing hot, and I had the air-conditioning cranked to the hilt. Max was napping in the back seat, and the cake was nestled on the front floor where it wouldn't fall. I sang along with the radio. The song, "So very hard to go" from Tower of Power was on, and I adore that song. I loved the disco era, and even though it was kind of a sad song, I always enjoyed singing it at the top of my lungs. I glanced down at the cake and hoped the lady liked it.

I drove down a long narrow street that was lined with lofty oak trees, their canopy shading the road in an old southern looking way, and then the voice told me that I had reached my destination on the left. I pulled into the driveway and saw one car parked in front of the garage. It was a very nice house, it was set on the bay, and I put the car in park beneath a grand oak tree and shut it off. I reached down and grabbed my purse, the cake, and then walked up the front steps. The door had a big wreath that was decorated with seashells on it, and there were two large urns filled with palms flanking each side. It was a beautiful house, and I rang the doorbell. I only had to wait for a minute, and the door swung open.

Justin stood there smiling at me, and behind him, a large Happy Birthday banner was hung on an entranceway to what looked like the kitchen. I looked at him shocked and asked if he had ordered a cake.

"My daughter called it in for me. I knew if you heard my voice, you'd know it was me. Come in, come in." He held out his hands for the cake, and I handed it over. My eyes looked around at the meticulous interior, and he told me to follow him, that he'd show me around.

"Whose birthday is it? I thought the kids went back home for school. Is it yours? If it is, then you and I share the same birthday. Now wouldn't that be funny? You never struck me as a Cancer. You're more Taurus or a Libra." He smiled and shook his head.

"My birthday isn't until October. It's your birthday. A little bird told me that the other day, and I thought, because you always do such a good job making me happy with the cookies, I'd treat you with a cake that I knew would be impeccable. With you making it yourself, how could it not be?" He chuckled and looked a little guilty, and I still couldn't believe he'd do this.

"I was going to ask you out to dinner, but I wasn't sure if you would go. I promise you though, I didn't mean any harm. I just wanted you to have a nice day. I know your daughter left again, and though I don't know you very well, I figured it to be just a nice gesture, that's all. I hope you're not mad." I shook my head no and laughed.

"Well, I know the cake will be amazing. Do you know how hard it is to get fresh pansies this time of year? I hope you like it. I know I definitely will. I was drooling the whole time it baked. That's so sweet of you, too, and yes, it's a little weird, but I think I'll survive your kindness."

He carried the cake into the kitchen and showed me around the house, not the bedrooms, just the lower floor. We walked out onto the terrace, and I realized his view was a lot like mine. He had a smaller pool than mine, but his landscaping was perfect.

"Would you like a glass of wine?" he asked, and I nodded yes. I walked around checking out the flower pots on the terrace, and he walked out with both red and white in his hands.

"What's your preference? I'm not sure what will go best with the cake, but I do have some hors d'oeuvres to snack on, just so you don't think I'm plying you with drink. I'll be right back with them, but what will it be, red or white?"

I told him white would be lovely, and I took a seat in an area that was set up with a coffee table and several rattan chairs with thick, comfortable cushions. I took a deep breath and tried to process it all. It was rather sweet of him to do all this just for my birthday. It made it very special, and he gained another two points in my book for being a nice guy.

Justin came back with a tray filled with cheeses, olives, mixed nuts, and some thinly sliced bread and tapenade. It looked lovely, and I could feel my stomach growling. I guessed there would be no pizza for me that night. He went back into the house and then materialized a minute later with an ice bucket, bottle of Chardonnay and two glasses. He uncorked the bottle and poured us each a glass and asked me what I had planned on doing before he had nixed it with his surprise. I laughed and told him that I was only planning to order a pizza on my way home and hang out with Max. With these snacks, I'd have no reason to now. He raised a glass and made a toast to my birthday, and I felt happy. I enjoyed his company, and though it could have, he didn't come across as a weirdo for his effort. I set my glass down and jumped up like I'd been scalded, almost sending the platter flying off the table.

I had forgotten Max! I got very anxious and felt a terror rise up in me as I checked my watch. It was so hot out, and I'd left my baby out in the car. I ran through the house as Justin followed me and sprinted out the front door to my car. Max was panting, sitting in the front driver's seat, and I unlocked the car and grabbed him. I held him close while I cried and told him how sorry I was.

Justin led me back inside and wet some washcloths to cool down Max's body, and I gave him a small amount of water. I sat him down on the floor, and he just looked at me with those sad eyes, his tongue was lolling about in his mouth as he panted, and his chest heaved as he took in the cooler air. I knew he'd been out there for around eight minutes. The car had been in the shade, but I had forgotten him. I knew then that I had to find out what was wrong with my head before something tragic happened.

A few minutes later, Max was moving around, and he seemed to be doing okay, but we moved the party inside where it was cooler. I told Justin about what had been happening lately with my forgetfulness. He was so understanding. He told me that he'd help me in any way that he could. I tried to calm down, and he left me alone for a few minutes so that I could compose myself. I sat there, petting Max, breathing deeply, in and out, and just calmed my mind with a meditation mantra running through my head. It helped me as it always did, and I stood up when I felt more relaxed. Justin was in the kitchen, and I asked him for another glass of wine. It was my birthday. I couldn't change what had happened. I could only move forward as I had done so many times before. If I got tipsy, I'd get an Uber home.

Justin had ordered a pizza for delivery while he was giving me the time to calm down. He felt bad about messing up my original plans, and we sat there grazing on his snacks and talking until the pizza arrived. He tipped the man at the door and carried a large box into the kitchen.

"I wasn't sure if you ate meat, so I opted for a Margherita pizza." I told him that it sounded fabulous, and it was one of my favorites. He told me about his wife then and what he had gone through with her cancer diagnosis and ultimate death from it. He was intent on living his life to the fullest capacity and in happiness. He wasn't over her yet, I could tell, but I think by talking to a woman who could understand, it gave him some comfort.

"Life is too short not to take advantage of the good it has to offer," he said with a smile, and I agreed wholeheartedly with his wisdom. I told him about my life with Alec and then about Raphael and that fiasco. We talked about my confusion, and he asked me if I had been feeling depressed. I had to think about it, but I could see where it could be a possibility. This past year had been crazy. I could see the signs here and there, and that there may be some grain of truth to it.

I'd been running myself ragged, and Justin suggested bringing up everything that had been happening to me mentally to my doctor and to not overreact. He had gone through something similar after his wife passed away, and it had turned out to be just an electrolyte imbalance, exhaustion and bit of depression. I hoped so, because the more scared I got, the more stress I brought on myself.

It was nice talking to him, and I found myself relaxing throughout the time we spent together. He brought out my cake an hour later with a single candle on top. He lit it up, and it was so pretty with the flowers adorning the flickering light. He sang to me, and he wasn't embarrassed about doing it in grand style. His voice was beautiful, and I made my wish and blew out the candle. This was a great way to spend my special day. Justin asked if I would be free in the future for a proper dinner, and I checked my phone and asked if Sunday was good for him. I had the day off and no plans, and I didn't want to have to rush after work to get ready.

I asked that we keep it casual, though. I didn't want it to be a fancy date. I preferred relaxed and not so intimate. I wasn't ready to date, and I could see with his lingering grief, he wasn't ready yet, either. I needed to get my head on straight before focusing on someone new in my life. He said that would be just perfect with him. He also asked if I'd be up to a field trip, seeing-as-how I was free all day, and I thought that might be fun.

I thanked him for the evening, grabbed Max, and headed off towards home.

Chapter Twenty Four

Stormy weather...and calming the seas of life.

When I got home, I walked through the doors and took a deep breath. I realized how much I loved this house, and there had been so many great memories made within these walls. Max stood beside me and gave me that funny doggy smile that he had when he was hungry. I fed him his food, and then we went out to watch the rest of the evening descend as the moon made its way above the sea. It was a beautiful crescent moon. It was sitting low in the sky, and it reflected off the slightly choppy water. Turning in the other direction, the storm clouds could be seen billowing in the distance. It was like a split scene, different in each one's own way.

The view was stunning, and I sat there with my buddy and wondered if Leila was seeing the same moon wherever she was on the trail. I figured, with the time difference, most likely not. I thought to myself how proud I was of her, and I'm in awe and so impressed with her tenacity to reach for her goals without batting an eye. We were alike in many ways, yet so different. My goals were much simpler, and I knew I was doing what I loved. The art of baking fueled my spirit, and the creation of items that brought so much joy to others left me feeling fulfilled.

I needed to believe in myself, knowing that I was comfortable with my choices. I didn't feel depressed, but perhaps I was. I just felt very worn out. I like to hope that the future would hold new experiences and new friends. I was already partway there.

The tropical storm didn't come until the middle of the night. I woke when the smoke alarms in the house beeped as the power went out, and I grabbed the flashlight out of the bedside table. Max sat alert next to me. I often enjoyed storms, the lighting crackling across the sky and the sound of the rumble of thunder that moves through you with that deep reverberation. The winds had picked up, and I went downstairs just to check on things. With the memory issues, I was finding I often double-checked things like the locks, the stove, and anything else I may have overlooked. I was trying to be more consciously present to see if it would help.

I stood in the living room and stared at the light show beyond the windows. It was incredible, the power of Mother Nature and what she can do. When the lighting lit up the sky, I could see the waves crashing over the rocks and knew we'd be in for a doozy of a storm. It was only supposed to last through tomorrow, but I had a roof over my head and felt safe.

The lightning lit the sky again, and a bolt of thunder rattled the windows. I jumped, and Max sat beside me, leaning against my leg. His hair was standing up on his back, and it made me uneasy. I hadn't seen him do this before, and storms never seemed to faze him. I leaned down and petted his head, cooing to him softly that everything would be all right, and then I heard glass breaking. Max started growling. It sounded as if it came from the side of the house.

"I hope a branch didn't come through the window," I told poor Max, and I slipped back upstairs to put on some slippers, carrying Max with me so that he didn't cut his feet. The alarm was beeping, and I shut it off and put Max in the bedroom. He wasn't happy with that, but his safety was my responsibility, and I didn't need to rush him to the vet during a storm with cuts on his paws.

I shined the flashlight beam around the living room when I got back downstairs and made my way over to the kitchen. The hallway that led to the garage was off the kitchen, and I could hear glass crackling in the side room that held the washer and dryer. I knew there was no tree outside of that window, and I started to feel nervous. It sounded like someone was in the house, and I stood there for a moment as my mind raced. I heard what sounded like someone banging into the dryer. I was sorry I turned off the alarm, and with the power out, I wasn't sure what good it would do anyway. I couldn't remember checking to see if the backup batteries were in need of replacing. I was assuming that the company took care of that when they came for annual maintenance, but it had beeped before I shut it down, so that must mean something.

I slipped back quietly to the kitchen and grabbed the biggest butcher knife I could find in the block. Break-ins in this neighborhood were rare, and I was grateful in a way that the girls weren't here. I backtracked to the living room and grabbed my purse. I felt around and found my cellphone. I didn't want to turn it on, because the light from the screen would give my location away to whomever was in there. I tiptoed up the stairs and locked myself in the bedroom with Max.

I switched my cell phone on, unsure if I'd get a signal in the storm, but prayed it would work. I dialed 911 and told the dispatcher that someone had broken into my home and gave her my address. I told the woman that I was locked in my bedroom upstairs and that someone was down in the laundry room. She told me to remain calm, and I took Max and hid in the closet. I waited for what seemed like an hour but was only ten minutes or so before I finally heard voices calling out to me. Someone was knocking on the bedroom door. I told Max to stay and locked him in there while I crept closer to the door.

It was the police. They asked if I was okay, and I told them that I was. I unlocked the door and was never so happy to see a cop in my life. They had apprehended a man in the living room; apparently, he was passed out on the couch. I told them I needed to get dressed and that I'd be right down. I was in my sheer pj's and an open robe, and I may have given them an unintentional show. I wasn't thinking straight, but it struck me that I should have actual clothes on when I reappeared. I'm sure they didn't care, but it just felt a little awkward. I grabbed some shorts and a tank top, put on a bra, and then let Max stay in the bedroom while I went downstairs.

I saw flashlights shining around the room and heard an angry voice raised to almost shouting. He was telling the police that he lived there. I knew that voice. It was Raphael.

"Ask her. I live here and take these goddamn cuffs off. For Christ's sake, I'm going to sue the department for this. I'll have all your badges. Gonna get you mother fuckers fired if it's the last thing I do. Tell them, Dest. Come on, baby. I'm sorry about everything. Let them know it's cool that I'm here." His words were slurred, and he looked at me with those big, sad pleading eyes.

He could have given Max a run for his money in the begging department. I wasn't having anything to do with it. I stood there shocked and watched as he fell sideways and smashed into my end table and toppled my favorite lamp. The police officer helped him up and pushed him towards the door.

"Do you know this man, ma'am?" I think I must have looked at the cop like he was crazy.

"I used to think I did, but he's a criminal, and from what I've been hearing, quite the con artist. He's never lived here, and I intend on pressing charges for trespassing and anything else you can come up with." I glared at Raphael, not understanding why he would break in and, for that matter, why he'd be drunk. He was never one to drink that much on a good day. The officer nodded and took notes, asking how I knew him and I told him what he had told me, who he probably lived with, being Mrs. Bromley, and that we'd been over for quite some time. He wasn't welcome in my house nor in my life.

Raphael was screaming at me by this point, calling me every name in the book, and I'd like to say that it didn't rattle me, but it did. The officer shoved him through the front door, and I could see the police lights in the pouring rain, flashing red and blue, blinding like a strobe at a disco. I turned away, visibly shaking, and went to get a broom and dustpan to clean up the glass.

The one policeman, Officer Cortez, walked around the outside of the house and looked for more damage. The broken window was all he found. Raphael had used a chair off the lanai to be able to climb through. I'm surprised that, if he had been that drunk, he didn't just break in through the French doors like a normal criminal probably would have done.

The power flickered once then came back on. I turned on the kitchen light and righted the table that Raphael had fallen on, and the lamp, thank God, wasn't damaged.

The other officer that I was familiar with, Harry Capellan, asked me if I had anything lying around the house to board up the window. I told him I had some wooden scraps out in the shed, but I hadn't seen the laundry room window, so wasn't sure if he had broken through the whole thing or just a section of it.

I knew Harry pretty well because he came in for cookies at least once a week. He was fit and must have worked out regularly because it was obvious that my cookies never made it to his hips. He was a sweet guy and was always so polite. I had asked him once how he could stomach being a cop, what with all the drugged-out derelicts and violent offenders, and he just smiled and told me that his dad had been a cop, so he was just carrying on the family tradition. He enjoyed most of it, disliked some aspects, but helping people was what he was born to do.

I was thankful that we had a good police force here, and he went out and found a piece of plywood big enough to block the brunt of the storm from coming in. I wasn't going to get much sleep, so I turned on the coffee pot. It was three a.m., and I figured maybe I'd skip out of work early tomorrow if I needed a nap. It was a light day, and with the girls, they could cover it. It would also depend on whether we had the power at the store.

Harry came back in when he was done, and I asked him if he wanted some coffee. He said he'd take one to go if that would be all right, and he went out to his cruiser to get his travel mug. I grabbed a dozen cookies out of the freezer and put them in a bag for him. With this humidity and heat, they wouldn't take long to defrost. He smiled when he saw what I was packing up, and I was happy for his help. Some things are just easier with a man around, but broken windows and dirt bag criminals weren't on my agenda for the night. I was happy for Harry being the kind of guy he was.

I poured his mug full, and he asked me if I had sugar, and I laughed at him.

"I'm the queen of sugar, sweetheart. Do I have sugar? What kind of fool question is that?" I laughed, and he blushed. I pulled out the bowl, and he scooped four heaping tablespoons into the coffee, and I smiled.

"With that much sugar, you're not going to need any cookies. But I'll give them to you anyway. You can take them to the precinct and share them with the boys if you want," I said as

238

I handed him the bag. I thought for a second and then went back into the freezer and grabbed another Ziploc filled with sugar cookies and added them to the snickerdoodles I had given him.

"Destiny, I think at least one of these packages won't make it back, but I'll be more than happy to share the other one with them. You are the best, and your cookies fuel a body well. Thank you. I appreciate it." He stood there as the water dripped off his hat and onto the floor. I handed him a towel to try to get some of it off his face and hair. I wasn't worried about the floor, knowing I still had the broken glass mess to clean up.

Harry showed me what he had done with the window. We chatted idly about the storm, and then he told me that Raphael had a laundry list of charges coming to him, including DWI. Apparently, his truck was down in the driveway. It was still warm, and how else could he have gotten here without driving it there? The keys had been found in his pocket, and he was going to be spending a few nights behind bars. I told Harry that I'd rearm the alarm system, and he told me that, even though I had turned it off, it had registered the alert with the company when Raphael had broken the window. The precinct had gotten a notification from the alarm company, but my 911 call reinforced the need for help.

He thanked me again and left. I went up and let Max out, after closing off the door to the laundry room. I'd clean up the glass once it was light out because I'm sure I'd miss a shard here and there. The power flickered again and went back out.

Max and I sat on the couch, and I pulled up some music on my iPad. I didn't want to burn out the phone in case the power stayed off for a long time, but I needed to hear some happy noise. I thought back over the day, again grateful for Justin and the cake, and now for Harry and his kindness. I had a good group of people surrounding me, and I smiled. I finished my coffee and went back in to pour myself another cup. Max was crashed out on the sofa, and I used the trusty flashlight to see what I was doing.

On the corner of the counter was a small blue business card. I turned it over and was surprised to find that it was Harry's. It had his personal cell phone number, his email address, and a note written neatly in black pen.

"If you need anything, give me a call. I promise I'll be right there." Anything was underlined twice, as was the word promise. I felt something foreign rise up within me, feelings that I hadn't thought about in way too long. An excitement was surfacing from the depths, and it was lighting me up like a billboard on a dark night. I realized that I was attracted to him in "that" kind of way.

I know he was a very nice guy from my previous interactions with him, and it didn't hurt that he was cute, too. I had never thought about him in any way other than a wonderful distraction when he came in to buy cookies, but my mind started pondering the possibilities. I felt myself becoming excited then wondered if I was taking his note in the wrong way.

You know me, my mind, and my insecurities. But thinking about it, I wondered if that's why he came in so often to buy cookies. I thought back over our interactions and thought that perhaps I wasn't imagining things after all.

I felt like a teenager, and I probably blushed, but only Max was there to see it. I looked over at my little love and giggled. I am a mermaid. We are a jolly sort, and when we have the world at our fingertips, we are especially happy.

The light beyond the window was moving into that morning shade of paleness tinged with pink, even with the rain and clouds; it was lovely to see. I was too excited to do anything other than sit with Max and think about what today may bring. I held Harry's card in my fingers and brought it up to my nose, inhaling the scent of his aftershave on it. I hoped it meant what I thought it did.

I was a single woman, and Justin was a dear soul. We had a lot in common, but now I had another option, and for some reason, the newest possibility brought me joy. I didn't have to settle for the first guy that had come in to my life. I could have many friends and take my time deciding which way my heart wanted to turn. It felt amazing. I dozed off for an hour or so then watched as the night turned into morning, gazing at the whitecaps that seemed to float on the crest of the waves.

It had been a tumultuous night, but something good had come of it. I hoped to be finally free of Raphael with this latest screw-up of his, and I was blessed to have made it through unscathed. I was strong, and I could chalk this up to another unexpected, yet interesting adventure. When one door closes, another eventually opens, and I was standing with waiting arms, ready to accept whatever may come. I was a mermaid after all. It's what we were born to do.

Chapter Twenty Five

Finding Joy in a new day that dawns.

I went to work the next morning a little early. I was slightly groggy from lack of sleep and figured I'd bake some cookies and then take the rest of the day off. I had the last dozen in the oven when Bonnie asked me if I wanted some company. I yelled up that it would be fine and was surprised when I looked up to see Harry walking through the door. He smiled at me, and I blushed.

He asked me if I was able to sleep after the break-in, and I told him I napped for a little on the couch, but that mostly, no good quality sleep. He had stopped by the house, thinking I would have taken the day off, and when I didn't answer, he came here. I was happy to see him, and it felt good to know he was concerned. He asked me if I'd like to skip out for a bit for lunch, and as my cookies were now done, I told him yes.

Harry was off duty and had his Jeep parked across in the City Hall lot, and we walked around the puddles that filled the parking lot from last night's storm. I smiled as he held the door for me while I climbed in. He didn't say anything about Raphael, and I thought that was good. Why mix business and pleasure? He turned down 41, and we went to Joy's Kouzine.

When we went inside, he chose us a table for four. It seemed like everyone working there said hello to him, so I knew he must be a regular. An extremely perky young lady waited on us. Her name was Joy, and she was the daughter of the owners. Her name fit her personality to a T. She reminded me of Leila. Her laughter and smile were contagious, and she was beautiful. We sat down, and I looked around at the other people who were dining. It seemed to be a very upbeat place. I looked at Harry and smiled.

"I've lived here for over twenty years, and I've never eaten here. From what I can see, it looks delicious." I sipped my iced tea and looked over the menu. They had French-style crepes, and I was dying to try one but decided to spend my carb intake on a chicken souvlaki pita instead.

Harry asked me about myself while we waited for our food, and I pretty much gave him the light-condensed version. I left out the Raphael part, because I just wasn't ready to rehash it yet. He told me about himself. He'd never been married but wasn't averse to it; he was just looking for the right one to come along. His standards were pretty high, he said, and working his shift, which was mostly nights, it didn't give him much time for socializing. He was trying to change shifts and had enough seniority now where he could.

"Let the young guys do it. I'm ready to give up the graveyard to the vampires," he said, and I laughed, imagining him patrolling the streets in a land reminiscent of *Night of the Living Dead*. I know most of Venice shuts down for the night at ten o'clock, since a lot of the people who live here are sixty-five and older. I told him what I was thinking, about the walking dead scenario, and he laughed.

"No, hon, those would be zombies; they eat people. Vampires suck your blood and you live forever." We were laughing when Joy brought us our food, and she asked what was so funny. We told her, and she joined in our merry conversation.

My lunch was amazing, and I knew that this would be a regular go-to place in the future. Maybe I'd even spot Harry here on one of his breakfast trips. I don't know why, but I was relaxed and felt like myself with him. He was close to my age, not bad on the eyes, and he had a great sense of humor. I still couldn't picture him being a police officer, though. They always seemed so gruff and serious. Harry was different, and it was refreshing. He finished up his Gyro, and I had the rest of my pita wrapped to go. It was a lot of food, and I knew, when I got home, I was going to dive bomb the internet to find a recipe for Tzatziki sauce. It was to die for. I could see that stuff perking up my boring salads, easily.

Harry paid the bill when we were done and left Joy a ten-dollar tip for lunch. She smiled and told me that it was nice to meet me, and her mother Alma peeked through the window, smiled brightly, and told Harry she'd see him soon. Yep, Harry knew the prime spots for high energy, great food, and good people. I told Joy that I'd be back next time to try the crepes. Maybe I'd try a bowl of the rice pudding, too.

We drove back to the island, and Harry pulled into the parking lot of the shop. I should have felt exhausted, but I was feeling good. He asked if he could see me again sometime, and I smiled and told him that would be wonderful. I meant it, too. I enjoy his company, and though not rushing to get back in a relationship, I think he knows that I'll be taking it slowly. He's a really good guy.

I walked into the shop and caught Bonnie on the floor playing with Max. She looked like she was having fun, and Max dropped his ball and came running over to me, trying to get a nose full of my take-out box, but I held it up out of reach. Bonnie said it had been brisk while I was gone, but she knew about last night and told me to go home and catch up on my sleep. I smiled and told her I just may do that. She's become like a mom to me, taking care of many things in the shop and always reminding me when I was working too hard to go out and take a break.

I gathered up my things and called Max, who came bounding over, happy to be heading home. I have to drive to work now that I'm bringing Max in unless I decide to look like Dorothy in *The Wizard of Oz* with Toto in the basket. Not that Max wouldn't mind. I'm sure he'd love it, but it's easier during the rainy months, and that way, I don't have a wet dog running around the store.

We got home, and I had an appointment that evening to get the window replaced. Everything was cleaned up, and Max and I went out to sit on the terrace. I watched the waves still roiled up and cloudy from the storm, and I said hello to Liam. For everything that happened, my mind was calm and in a place of peace. I wasn't afraid of what tomorrow or the next day would bring. I guess I'm content; yes, content describes it perfectly.

I don't feel lonely. I just feel like I'm finally in a place where I'm drifting with a purpose. It's not aimless; there is a destination in mind when I see my life. The ocean lays before me like a gorgeous blue-green carpet, and I know I could walk right out there, dig my toes in the sand, and feel that cool wetness flow over me, and I would be alive, cleansed and beautiful. I've become everything I ever wanted for myself. Accomplished, true, free, and beautiful. I am a mermaid, I'll always be a mermaid, and there's nowhere else I'd rather be than right here, right now, and in love with this wild and crazy thing called my life.

Epilogue

Leila and Julia were married on the beach by a close friend of theirs from overseas. The wedding was perfect, the weather amazing, and it brought me bittersweet memories of my wedding so long ago with Alec. I had embraced the good times of my life with him and let go of the rest. I forgave him for being human, because forgiving would be the saving grace for my soul.

The wedding was held a year after they returned from their trip. I've never seen two souls more in love than those girls. There were around fifty of their friends in attendance, and we had a reception planned at Fins afterward. I cried when they said their I do's, and I looked at my beautiful ocean.

It was one of those stunning days when the sea was calm, and I smiled when one rogue waved came ashore and touched down lightly at my feet and deposited a shell that seemed, from an angle, to look like a heart. I knew it was Liam. He was always here for me, and he knew how to tug at my heart strings at just the right time. The sun was still just slightly above the horizon as the newlyweds kissed, and as the big bright orb sunk below view, the green flash was there for just one moment before it disappeared from view.

I looked over and held up my camera, catching the moment of the flash and their kiss. After checking to see if I captured it, I was impressed with its raw beauty. Once I blow it up and frame it, it will be a perfect gift for them. I chose not to show it to them right away. I'm keeping it as a surprise.

I have so much to be thankful for. My life is a blessing, and Max was home waiting. He wasn't allowed on the beach, and I don't think a lot of the folks would have appreciated his doggy prints on their shoes.

"Are you ready to go, sweetness?" I smiled as I felt his arms come from behind me, and I leaned back as his lips nuzzled me in that light, sweet way that he had.

"Let me just stand here for a moment longer. I'm not ready to let it go yet," I said as I turned for a second to smile at him.

"At times like these, I wish that I could pluck these moments up and slip them into my pocket for gray days."

I breathed in the air. The freshness of salty and tangy mixed with his aftershave was like a sweet dream to my senses. I closed my eyes and opened them again as the day turned into a dusky darkness. The moon was already climbing; it was full and lush and blindingly bright. It was perfect.

We stood there just being, and I was content right here, locked in his arms. He kissed me on the ear and turned me around again. He was looking into my eyes, that deep passion he always had surrounding him like a cloud of goodness. It was in everything that he did, and it's what I loved most about him. I always felt like I was swimming when I dove into the depths of those blue eyes. He had captured this mermaid's heart, and I had gladly turned it over to his loving touch. I know now what love is, and I am blessed to have found it with this beautiful soul.

"Come on, Harry. I think I'm ready to go now. I guess we don't want to keep the party waiting," I said to him, and he kissed me lightly on the cheek. His fingers were stroking the sides of my face as he looked at me like I was the most important thing in the world. He kissed me then, passionately, lovingly, and I met him in the middle of the depths of this beautiful affair with everything that I had, a mermaid swimming in an ocean of love, alive and beautifully whole.

The End

Author Bio

Kimberly L. Laettner is a published author and native of Hamburg, New York. She moved to Venice, Florida to pursue her dream of writing novels and to enjoy life in paradise with her number-one fan and retired husband, Jeffery.
They have three, four-legged furry children.

Kimberly is a poetry blogger on Wordpress and can be found at zipsrid.wordpress.com. She has over four thousand followers. Diary of a Middle-Aged Mermaid is her second work of fiction.

Made in the USA
Columbia, SC
22 February 2021